THE
PRIMAL KEY

BY
C.A. HARTLEY

STYXERS✠BOOKS

Text Copyright © 2016 by C.A. Hartley
Cover and Interior Art © 2016 by C.A. Hartley

First Edition, August 2016
2 4 6 8 10 9 7 5 3 1

Identifiers: LCCN 2016912065 | ISBN 978-1-945471-09-4 (paperback)

For C.J.

Special thanks to
Owen, Bradley, Drew
and M&D

CONTENTS

CHAPTER ONE

THE LAST UNPACKED BOX

Just past midnight Anne Clarke crept across the uneven attic floorboards. Mom had told her to leave the box alone. She even banned her from the attic, but Anne couldn't let it go. She itched to know what was inside. For the first time, something mysterious involved her, instead of Alex. Brushing a few copper strands of hair from her eyes, she took a calming breath and ripped off the packing tape. The cardboard split, spilling an iron letterbox and books on the floor.

Anne selected a book from the pile and puffed dust off its faded leather cover. It stung her eyes. She muffled a cough and several sneezes in her sleeve. Did anyone hear? She listened, expecting Mom's startled shout. The only noise came from Alex's

1

room — snoring. She returned her attention to the book entitled, *Pieter Bruegel the Elder's Child's Play: Dangers Lurking in the Alleyway*, by Matthew Clarke. These were her father's journals, she realized. Mom seldom spoke of Anne's father and, when she did, tears flowed.

Anne's heart beat faster as she reached for another book. This time she wiped the cover against her sweatshirt to avoid another dust storm. The title, *Responsible Art: Avoiding Deadly Results*, fascinated her, but before she opened the book, Alex's snoring turned to groaning. She was running out of time. Alex would wake up from his dream screaming, or maybe singing or even chanting. After Mom calmed him, she would discover Anne's bed empty. Anne stacked the journals in a pile and placed the box's cardboard remains over them. Tomorrow she would find a way to smuggle the books to her room. She picked up the metal chest; something clunked inside it. A quick peek; I have time, she told herself.

Fingers trembling, she flipped the latch. Inside a tarnished silver paperweight rested on scrunched envelopes addressed to her father. She nudged the silver ball aside, picked up the first and stared at his name. I shouldn't open it, Anne thought, as she turned the envelope over. Sealed? Nope. No one will find out. She carefully slipped out the letter.

Dear Matthew,

The twins will be born tomorrow. I've named them Alex and Anne, as we planned. Selena and Marcus flew in last week to help me. Mother offered to come. I told her to stay at the estate. She

2

would provide no comfort for me. She's obsessing over Collective business and Alex. She has already created a training schedule for him. She's sure he will prove himself worthy of leading the Collective and continuing her quest to connect the gemstone tablets. Mother wants us to move back to the estate so she can train the twins. I refused. I'm terrified she will sense Anne's potential and push her too hard, too fast. I can't bear the thought of losing her.

Matthew, I feel Anne's talents growing inside me just as I sensed your abilities when we first met. Until you teach her to use the Crazy Keys safely, I will do everything I can to ground her in the present, keep her out of the past and seal off the future. If she becomes unstable before you return, Selena and Marcus will help her disappear so she can develop her talents in seclusion.

Even though I lost you three months ago, my heart still fills with hope when my comm-pad chimes. So I write these letters. I don't know where to send them; you'll never receive them. Please find your way back. I can't raise the twins without you.

Forever yours,
Elizabeth

Anne read the letter again trying to make sense of it. Mom's wrong, she decided. She was already thirteen. The family's abilities would have shown up by now. She remembered when Alex's skills emerged. He was three. Grandmother was thrilled. She even gave him an official title: The Amalgamator. Anne thought the name sounded like a turbocharged garbage disposal, which — when Alex ate — pretty much summed him up.

Anne sighed. Everything revolved around Alex, even where they lived. At least their latest stop — Collinsville, Illinois — was tolerable. The brick library's selection of art books was reasonable and the 170-foot ketchup bottle made her laugh every time she biked past it. Alex still took creepy fieldtrips, but Prehistoric Cahokia, America's first city, seemed safer than the Los Angeles La Brea Tar Pits. They lived in Collinsville a little over a year, long enough for Anne to consider making a few friends. But having friends led to painful goodbyes when "Collective business" or Alex's training forced them to move — again.

Mom knew Anne was lonely and tried her best to cheer Anne's spirits. While Alex roamed through the Cahokia Historic Site chatting with people who died a thousand years ago, Mom and Anne would relax on a grassy mound and sketch, play cards or gaze at clouds. Occasionally, Mom would share a story from the time before — before Dad disappeared.

Anne stared at the letters. As much as she wanted to know Dad, this wasn't the right way. As she moved them aside, beneath the last letter, she found *Grandpa's Crazy Keys*, by Hubert Browning, her grandpa. "I thought I lost you." She cradled the book, as if welcoming a long-lost friend. The book's poems described the discovery of Grandmother's five gemstone tablets — tablets covered with bizarre symbols and spells. As a child, she sat on Grandpa's lap as he read and Anne pretended to travel to the ancient civilizations each crazy key poem unlocked.

Other than Mom, he was the only one who paid attention to her. She opened her old friend and read the first poem aloud.

I've made a bracelet of five crazy keys
And hidden secret clues within my verse.
Unravel them to open doors with ease.
Beware! What you find can cast a curse.
Behind doors cryptic, mystic arts reveal
The nature of all things, allowing you
To nurture life, evolve, protect and heal.
In time, perhaps, you'll make the next breakthrough.
If you are stuck behind my doors and find
Your way is lost, then spot my little sign.
The pictures 'round the poems keep in mind.
What's in each room and in my book align.
Turn pages now to read my simple rhyme.
Follow our quest and travel 'round in time.

For Anne, Grandpa's poems always led to grand — though imaginary — adventures. She held the book at arm's length. What would Dad teach me to do with your Crazy Keys? She drew it closer to study the illustrations around the poem, searching for anything even remotely dangerous. When she inspected Thoth's Egyptian temple, her heart fluttered. At first, the vibration felt pleasant like the quivering she sometimes experienced when sketching in her journals, but it intensified, twisting painfully and rattling her body. Earsplitting ringing and a zillion images bombarded her mind. As the blaring diminished, the images dissolved into a single scene — a woman painting illustrations for *Grandpa's Crazy Keys*.

"Grandmother Isadora? But how?" Anne asked.

The woman pushed back from her drawing table, scraping her chair across the floor. "Who's there?"

Before Anne made sense of what was happening, Grandmother's image faded, leaving Anne in darkness. In the distance, an electric blue bolt danced toward Anne. As the bolt sizzled nearer, the hair on her neck tingled.

"I've found one," she heard a man say. "This one's huge."

"About time," a woman answered. "It's the girl. Contain her — quickly!"

The bolt split, surrounding Anne. A stray bolt lashed against Anne's arm sending an electric shock jolting through her body and bringing her to her knees. Trapped in a bubble of ozone-laced air, she gasped, desperate to escape.

"Your modulations are wrong! She can't escape," the woman yelled at the man.

Although Anne sensed cruelty in her voice, the face that appeared outside the bubble was beautiful and smiling. Her long blonde hair flowed in a gentle breeze, a breeze Anne ached to suck into her lungs, but couldn't.

"Take my hand and the pain will stop," she promised. "I'll help you."

Confused and scared, Anne reached for the woman, but as her hand touched the mesh barrier, energy scorched her fingers. She recoiled, clutching her hand against her chest.

The woman's welcoming smile turned sour as she glared

impatiently at Anne. "It will only hurt for a moment. You must push through."

The man's pudgy face appeared near the dome. "She won't make it in time. You must leave her."

She shoved him away and turned to Anne. "I can't keep the dome intact much longer. You'll be lost."

"Lost!" Anne panicked. She gathered her strength and jumped toward the woman. Intense heat burned her skin as she reached the dome's edge. Something struck her. The dome imploded, and Anne landed in a heap on a cold, wet cement path.

CHAPTER TWO

ALEX'S RUDE AWAKENING

Mom's yell jolted Alex awake. "Anne's gone!"

"She's sneaking around in the attic." Alex grumbled, kicking off the blanket. "What's the big deal? Anne never does anything dangerous. She only writes and draws in those stupid journals."

Anne loved art and, as long as her compositions kept improving, Grandmother Isadora stayed off her back. Anne was lucky she hadn't inherited weird, spooky abilities. She had fun with Mom while he trained — nonstop. Grandmother insisted he visit mystics who communicated with the dead or read past lives, and he spent hours studying ancient languages in the off chance some dead person saw the Carnelian Tablet intact. That's why Grandmother pushed him hard. He was her best chance to find the broken pieces and unlock the Carnelian Tablet's secrets.

"Listen to me!" Mom insisted. "Anne fell into an unstable portal."

"But, how —"

"Seth locked on to the portal's pattern. The entry point is still active in the attic. Grab your essentials and get to the safe-room. Don't open the door for anyone!"

"What about you?"

"I'll try to lure Seth's agents away from the house. When they're gone, contact Marcus and find Anne. Promise me you'll protect her. She needs you more than she knows." She gave him a quick hug.

Alex knew the drill. He slipped on jeans and his favorite sneakers. Into his backpack, he placed his father's leather jacket, a game tablet, and a few issues of *Mad Magazine*. He grabbed Anne's backpack and hurried to the attic, pulling up the retractable stairs behind him. He crossed the attic to the old bookcase in the far corner and pulled on the third shelf. It cracked open. Alex frantically ran his hand across the unfinished wall hiding the safe-room door.

"Come on, come on, come on . . . . Why did Mom pick such a dark corner?" His hand brushed over the metal label inscribed with his initials. The wall opened into a long, narrow room. As Alex locked the door, a sign listing the safe-room's specifications illuminated:

Blast and Ballistic Safe Door
Air Filtration System: Chemical and Biological Gases

Alternate Power Source
Surveillance Command Center
Waste Disposal System
30-Day Food and Water Supply

Alex sighed. Thirty days? Would he be stuck here that long? Last time Seth's spies tracked them down in Los Angeles, Alex had five minutes to fill a backpack and flee. Since then he kept his backpack with the essentials ready, just in case.

On the wall by the door, a red switch glowed. He flipped it and the wall lit up, displaying the rooms in the house. The back door, window broken, stood open. Seth's men were already inside ransacking their way through the house. Alex watched a man overturn his mattress, crashing it onto his dresser. The intruder heaped everything in the closet onto the floor. "Nothing," he said to the men in the hallway. "Go check the attic," he ordered, before punching holes in the wall with a crowbar.

Two men waited in the hall while a third unfolded the attic steps. Alex retreated further into the safe-room as the men climbed the stairs. They immediately headed toward the bookcase. Alex kicked himself for leaving it ajar. The largest man hit the safe-room door with a hatchet. The plywood splintered, but the door held. After a dozen swings, he gave up, and Alex exhaled the breath he didn't realize he was holding.

The men retreated to the far side of the attic. As gunshots ricocheted off the door, Alex pressed his back against the wall. The bullets stopped, and the men left the attic, bulldozing their way through the house to the living room.

A woman, carrying a metal case joined them. "Did you find

it?" she asked, pulling little bricks out of the case and connecting them with wire.

"No. The boy holed up in a safe-room in the attic. Bruegel's ball may be in there with him."

"Then we're done here. We captured the mother and Lamia is closing in on the girl. Seth wants Bruegel's ball destroyed and the boy eliminated."

Moments after they left, an explosion rocked the safe-room. Alex screamed, covering his ears with his hands. The screens blipped out, except the view from the shed. I'm going to die, he thought, looking at the fiery remains of the house. He squeezed his eyes shut, his body trembling as he slid down the wall to the floor, waiting for the safe-room to plummet into the basement. Mom . . . their house . . . everything was gone!

Something brushed his shoulder. His brain told him to run, but his body wouldn't. He crawled toward the door, despite the destruction on the other side.

"Alex, wait!"

"Aunt Selena? Wh-where? How?" he mumbled, unable to say more.

"We must leave. The safe room's foundation can withstand a blast, but they'll target the support structure next. Where's Elizabeth?"

Alex swayed. He leaned against the wall to steady himself. "Sh-sh-she tried . . . . They took her."

"We'll get her back." She scanned the room, her eyes lingering on some old books and a metal box. She opened the box, grabbed a silver ball and dropped it into Alex's hand. "Keep this safe." She tossed the stack of journals into a duffle bag. "Time to go."

Alex shouldered the two backpacks — his and Anne's. He heard a faint ringing as they stepped through the wall and into Selena's house on the outskirts of Seattle, Washington. Selena guided Alex through the kitchen and out the back door and nodded toward a beat-up, pale-blue Volkswagen bug. "Seth probably anticipated a portal escape and might track us. From now on, we travel the old-fashioned way. Next stop's the King County Airport."

Once they were on the highway, Alex leaned his head against the car window and zoned out, watching the headlights illumine the white line on the road.

"Call Marcus," Selena said to the car's comm-panel.

Marcus's voiced asked, "Where are you?"

"Seattle. I have Alex, but they took Elizabeth."

Marcus remained silent.

Keeping his eyes glued on the white line, Alex whispered, "They didn't even want me. They wanted Anne. Everything else Seth told them to destroy. Will he kill Mom, too?"

"Elizabeth is too valuable a prize," Marcus answered.

"Bring Anne to the safe house," Selena said. "We'll meet you there and figure out how to help Elizabeth."

"No, we're going to the estate," Marcus insisted. "Alex is the Amalgamator and Anne —"

"Blast the Collective!" Selena pounded the steering wheel. The car swerved into the other lane and cut off a semi. The driver blared the air horn, startling Alex. Selena ignored it and hit the accelerator.

Alex pressed deep into the seat and grasped the side of the door. "Mom told me to protect Anne. She made me promise."

12

Selena clenched the steering wheel tightly and glared straight ahead.

Marcus pounced on her hesitation. "Until Elizabeth returns, the estate is the only safe place for the kids. When you land in New York, a Collective driver will take you to the Metropolitan Museum of Art."

"Is The Met secure?" Selena asked.

"We added it to our collection last year. Meet me in the Douglas Dillin Boardroom."

"Fine," Selena snapped and ended the call.

Selena drove on in silence. At the airport, Selena spoke briefly with the pilot before joining Alex in the jet's plush passenger section.

"You'll be busy tomorrow, and need to rest," she said. "The bedroom is in the rear."

Alex placed Anne's backpack on the floor and tossed his own onto the bed. Above him, the plane's air vents blasted cold air. "I'm coming, Anne," he said and wrapped himself in his father's leather jacket.

14

CHAPTER THREE

SAN NICOLO'S DOORWAY

As Anne rolled out of the muddy puddle, she saw what — or rather who — had hit her.

A woman with black spikey hair groaned as she stood. "That was too close," she said as she brushed dirt off her jeans and leather jacket. "Bixia." She stated her name.

Anne heard the woman's words, but they didn't make sense. Anne's heart pounded, rushing oxygen to her brain. Her legs turned rubbery as the ground twisted and tilted. Bixia caught her, easing her down.

"Try to relax," Bixia encouraged her. "Take slow, deep breaths."

Gradually, the world settled. "Wh-wh-where am I?" Anne

asked. Although ground fog obscured everything beyond a few feet, she heard city traffic.

"We're in Central Park. That portal almost killed us. I thought we were done for."

Anne had heard about portals. Grandmother Isadora created them to allow the Collective to move unnoticed around the world. But how did a portal to New York City open in her attic? Mom insisted on a portal-free home. Anne tried to piece together what happened. "That beautiful woman must have created the portal. She tried to help me escape, but I couldn't reach her."

"Beautiful? Try deadly. She's Seth's newest top agent. Remember her face. When you see her again — run."

Anne never met Seth, but she hated him. He had stolen Grandpa from her. When Grandpa refused to share the Collective's secrets, Seth murdered him. Since then, Seth's agents relentlessly hunted Anne's family. She searched the tree-lined, park path for a hiding place.

"We can't stay here too long," Bixia said, pulling Anne to her feet. "I want you with Emma before his agents arrive. She'll protect you until you reach the Collective's estate."

Anne thought of Mom's letter. She didn't want Anne near the estate or alone with Grandmother Isadora. "I can't go there," she blurted out.

"You got that right. You're too hot. Come on. I'll try to put Seth's agents off our track."

She followed Bixia down a dim pathway, and up stone steps leading to an octagon plaza with a six-story obelisk in the center. Pigeons scattered in a frenzy of squawks, flapping wings and stray feathers as Bixia circled the monument.

"What are you doing?" Anne asked, brushing her hands through her hair and dusting her shoulders, hoping she wouldn't find pigeon poop.

"This is Cleopatra's Needle. It marks an entrance to our transportation network. We stopped using the Needle after it dumped us in Egypt."

"Egypt is better than facing Seth's agents." Anne joined Bixia and reached out to touch the obelisk.

"Back off," Bixia said, slapping Anne's hand away from the monument. "It won't work. You opened a massive portal at your house. It redlined our detection grid and activated the security system. The direct portals to the estate are on lockdown until Isadora reestablishes the links." Bixia shook her head. "I can't believe your mom let you experiment on your own."

Anne laughed nervously. "I . . . I created a portal? Only Transcenders can create portals. I'm not . . . ." Anne's legs weakened again.

She envied Alex's skills and the attention Grandmother lavished on him. Sometimes, while she watched Alex train, she imagined becoming a Healer or an Alchemist like her mom, but becoming a Transcender was out of the question. They were rare, secretive members of the Collective — spies and special messengers. They lived dangerous lives. Most died young — or worse — disappeared without a trace.

"I didn't mean to open it," she whispered. "Everything closed in around me. I panicked."

"Portal Protocol #1: Panicky portals produce pandemonium," Bixia recited. She glanced up at the obelisk with satisfaction.

Faint musical tones made Anne's chest flutter again. She

backed away from Bixia and her portal. "But you said the portals are shut down."

"They are. I put my energy pattern on the obelisk. If we're lucky, Seth's agents will think we took a portal out of here."

They followed a path through a tunnel and past a deserted playground. When they reached a huge building, Bixia opened a metal door and pushed Anne inside. The air tasted musty, like an old library basement, and the woman Bixia approached resembled the librarian in Collinsville. "Take Anne to a shielded office. Keep her there until her energy pattern fades."

"I'll take care of her," Emma said.

As Emma steered her down a long narrow hall, Anne overheard Bixia say, "I have the package. Your granddaughter created the portal."

Isadora wasn't a warm or doting grandmother but, until now, Anne didn't fear her. "I should call home," Anne said as casually as she could manage.

"For your mother's safety and yours, you must wait until morning," Emma said. "Now, let's get you settled." She led Anne to a cramped, book-cluttered room.

Anne smiled in relief. Marcus, Mom's childhood friend was waiting there.

"Your energy pattern is off the charts," he said, placing his hands on her shoulders. "You need rest, and I won't let you do anything else unprotected."

His grip tightened, and Anne stiffened as Emma aproached with a syringe and stuck the tranquilizer into Anne's shoulder. "Picture a beautiful beach with a gentle breeze and rhythmic surf."

Instead, Anne imagined huge, angry waves pounding the sand — then nothing.

In the morning, Anne awoke with a throbbing headache and a stiff neck. She was still in the cell-like office, and her jailer, Emma, waited at the door.

"I have fresh clothing for you and fruit for breakfast."

"Is the food drugged?" Anne asked, trying to make her words as venomous as possible.

Emma calmly placed the breakfast tray on the desk, ignoring or dismissing Anne's nasty tone. "No, dear, the fruit is organic. You have ten minutes to eat and change clothes before we leave for the estate. Alex and Selena are traveling with us."

"Is Alex here?" Anne's spirits began to improve. If Alex was going with her, Mom must know what happened.

"He's on his way." Emma replied as she left, locking the door behind her.

Anne examined the clothing. She preferred peg-leg jeans. Still, baggy pants beat her mud caked sweats. She gave the fruit a poke. It looked fresh, and hunger won out. The food helped settle her stomach and clear lingering tranquilizer fog from her mind. By the time she finished the orange juice, her fear and anger began to mingle with curiosity and anticipation. In a few hours, she would be at the estate. Maybe Mom would join them.

Emma returned and led Anne through a drab hallway. "I know last night was rough, but you're in the safest building we own outside the estate. The Metropolitan Museum of Art is our finest stronghold."

Anne begged Mom to bring her to the city to see the museums, but the trip she imagined included the Plaza hotel and pastries from *Lady M Cake Boutique*.

The drab hallway opened into a reception area bustling with museum-goers. Emma walked past the ticket kiosk and the education center to a stairway leading to the Greek art galleries. At the top, they entered an airy hall. A huge marble column dominated the room.

"Wow! Where did they find that?" Anne asked.

"That's the column's top," Emma explained. "In its proper location at the temple, it was raised fifty-eight feet up. We found a nice home for it where people can appreciate its delicate carving. The Met received it as a gift from the American Society for the Excavation of Sardis."

"How do you know?" Anne asked.

"I am the museum's director. Collective members manage the great museums. I'm also a Transcender — a master of the Crystal Tablet — which is now part of your fate as well."

"You're a master? And you drugged me?"

"Keep your voice down, dear. You'll draw attention." Emma firmly gripped Anne's arm. "Let's keep moving, shall we?"

Anne yanked out of her grasp and strode into the next gallery. Its magnificence stunned her. Light streamed from skylights in the barrel-vaulted ceiling, illuminating the twice-life-size marble and bronze statues, athletes and warriors. As she wandered through the exhibit, the charm slowly faded. She didn't understand why, but the statues in their varying degrees of ruin, saddened her. Anne turned to a display case filled with terracotta jars. As she looked at the first jar, a lump formed in her throat.

"Theseus is slaying the Minotaur," Emma said, joining her. "Are you familiar with the story?"

Anne nodded, staring at the half-man-half-bull Minotaur. "A few adults made a stupid mistake, and innocent kids paid for it with their lives."

The myth repulsed Anne. In the version she hated most, jealous sports fanatics killed King Minos's son because he won too many contests hosted by Aegeus of Athens. Furious and heartbroken, Minos declared war on Athens. In retribution for his son's death, Minos demanded seven Athenian boys and seven Athenian girls travel to Crete. Once there, Minos threw the kids a party before locking them in the Labyrinth at Knossos where the Minotaur lived. They soon lost their way in the endless passageways and the Minotaur devoured them. Theseus joined the third group of kids making this sacrificial journey. With Ariadne's help, he killed the Minotaur and found his way back to the gate. Even though the Minotaur ate the kids, Anne pitied him — locked up in the Labyrinth — despised and alone. It wasn't his fault he was born a monster.

Anne heard quick steps behind her and, when she turned, saw Marcus.

"I thought we were meeting you —" Emma began to say, but Marcus shook his head and motioned them away from the crowd into the adjoining gallery. He brushed his hand across the base of his skull; blood streaked his fingers and trickled down his neck, staining his shirt collar. Marcus looked at his fingers with disgust and wiped them on his pants.

A man in the main hall yelled, "Watch it!"

Marcus peered around the display case. "I swore I lost them in the park!" he hissed. "Lamia's men are here. Take Anne to the doorway. I'll find Alex."

Emma grabbed Anne's arm and pulled her with surprising strength through the main gallery. Anne tripped, but regained her balance, as Emma herded her past two guards and into the Great Hall, the main entrance to the museum. Emma whisked Anne past the people lined up to buy tickets. At the base of the Great Stairs, they veered left into a narrow gallery and past a huge processional cross. Abruptly, Emma stopped, facing an open, stone door.

"This is the doorway from the Church of San Nicolò," Emma explained, as if it might mean something to Anne. "Go on. Walk through."

Anne glanced at the stone lions guarding the arched door. She peered through to the other side. The gallery containing ivory statues and stained glass windows appeared innocent enough.

"Hurry," Emma urged. "The portal is stable. It modulates. Lamia can't trace it."

Anne clutched her stomach, remembering the pain from her first portal. "Where does it lead?"

Emma nudged her forward. As Anne passed through the door toward the checkered black-and-white tile floor and the exhibits beyond, she heard ringing like wind chimes during a storm. Her skin prickled and her teeth chattered. She tried to retreat, but the lights brightened, blurring everything. Her breath caught, squeezed tight in her lungs. Then the light faded.

"You're safe," a woman assured her. She grasped Anne's hands and guided her into a tunnel with charcoal walls brightening, at the far end, to dazzling silver. Anne expected to feel cold, but found the passage welcoming. A clean, slightly bitter aroma, like cocoa, replaced the stale museum air. As the light increased, her guide's features became clear. An older woman with braided dark brown hair, streaked with gray, smiled at Anne.

"Grandmother Isadora!"

"Call me Isadora. You know the grandmother thing is your mother's doing. I refuse to admit I'm old enough for grandchildren."

The hallway brightened and Anne noticed elaborate engravings on the metal walls. Isadora pressed her hand against the symbols. "This is Epi-Olmec script — common in Mexico around 100 BCE. After you're settled, you may explore your links to this culture."

Anne tried to contain her anxiety, but failed. "Lamia attacked Marcus. He went to find Alex. We have to help them. What if something happens to Alex . . . ?"

"Marcus will take care of him. Going back to The Met would complicate matters. For now, I think recent events call for tea and a quick chat." Although a wall blocked the end of the hall, Isadora didn't slow. Anne heard the now-familiar ringing as they passed through the portal into an office filled with art, antiques and books.

Isadora smiled and crossed the room to pour the tea. "I can't believe I missed noticing your talents. I've always been good at finding Transcenders. Your first 'approved' time travel through San Nicolò's doorway went well. Transcending is simple really — a little hop across a fold in time. You managed it in fine fashion." Isadora laughed. "Of course, the doorway is buffered, unlike the sloppy, nasty portal you created last night. Frankly, I'm surprised you survived." She handed Anne a teacup. "Jasmine settles my nerves."

"Is it made of abalone shells?" Anne asked, admiring the cup.

"No, Tiffany glass. You do have an eye for fine art. I believe the cup is as important as the tea. Don't you?"

Anne sipped her tea. "Is Mom on her way?"

Isadora huffed. "Elizabeth is foolish. She pushed her training aside and then put her children in danger. I told her she was taking too great a risk."

"Where's Mom?"

"Seth traced your portal. His men destroyed the house, and captured Elizabeth."

Anne's teacup shattered on the floor. "Everything is gone? And Mom?" Her eyes opened wide with realization. "It's my fault!"

"We will bargain for Elizabeth's life," Isadora said. "Seth hasn't made his demands yet, but it won't take long."

"Demands? Like a ransom?"

"Yes, but Seth won't want money. He covets the Collective's secrets. We'll wait to see what he asks."

What if Seth asks too much, Anne wondered. Would Isadora still make the trade or sacrifice her own daughter to protect the Collective? Anne didn't know. If it came to it, she would rescue Mom herself.

Chapter Four

The Magical Stela

Alex followed his aunt through The Met's second floor galleries. He didn't notice the art on the walls, or stop to admire the Spanish courtyard, or even glance down into the European sculpture garden. Selena ushered him into an elevator and pressed number four. Alex leaned against the wall. *How can I keep Anne safe? I'm not the best brother*, he admitted to himself.

Sometimes, when he practiced communicating with the dead, he would send ghosts to tease her. They would slam Anne's door, cry out from her closet or throw her journal on the floor — cheap parlor tricks. She found none of it even remotely funny. She especially hated when Alex threatened to enter one of her past lives. It was a threat he held for extreme situations — like not ratting on him when he skipped studies to play video games. He didn't want to be in her lives anymore than she wanted to share them. Alex thought back to the first and only time he trespassed on Anne's lives — it wasn't pretty.

✠✠✠✠✠

Anne and Alex were nine and living with Mom in Spain. Grandmother flew in to supervise his week-long, intensive training session. The first day, Alex successfully entered a meditative trance, traversed his own past and returned with a few memories intact.

Proudly, he announced, "I had six past lives!"

Grandmother smiled sympathetically. "Not everyone can be an old soul."

He remembered the fragments — like snapshots — of his former lives, and was sure he had once lived in ancient Greece. He was about to insist he was in fact an old soul, when Anne, who was sketching at a table, snickered and snorted.

"Anne, do you have something you want to share?" Grandmother asked in a way that meant she expected Anne to say 'no' and quietly return to her sketch.

To Alex's amazement, Anne bolted up and asked, "Alex, were you always a boy or were you ever a girl in your past lives?" Anne tried to contain her smile but failed and burst into giggles.

Alex's ears warmed as his face reddened.

"Why don't you join us," Grandmother patted a spot for Anne on the floor beside her. "Alex's next lesson is sharing his memories with others. Come see for yourself."

Anne lingered for a moment, her eyes studying the spot on the floor before joining them.

Alex didn't want to share his lives with Anne. He glared at her, but she didn't return his gaze — her eyes fixed on the carpet.

"Alex, take Anne's hand," Grandmother instructed.

Alex squeezed Anne's fingers tighter than necessary. She winced, gave him an icy stare and dug her nails into his skin. I'll show her, he thought. Even if Grandmother noticed the tension between them, Alex was betting she wouldn't stop the lesson.

Grandmother tapped Alex's shoulder letting him know it was time to start his meditation. "Think of a vivid memory from one of your lives. The ones with strong emotions are the easiest to share."

As she had taught him, Alex cleared his mind, focusing on a single emotion — humiliation. This time, instead of reflecting on his own past lives, he reached into Anne's soul. Into his consciousness floated the image of a young woman chained to a post. She was weeping and her shame and disgrace washed over Alex. An angry crowd taunted her and, as their first stone struck, she tried to curl into a ball, but chains held her tight. More stones hit their mark. She screamed, thrashing against her chains, desperate to escape.

Anne yanked her hands away from Alex, a look of horror was in her eyes. She drew her knees up to her chest and hugged them.

"Too much for you?" Grandmother asked Anne. "Accepting past lives from others can be difficult. Uncle Wayne can work with Alex for the rest of the day. Go find him, then you may return to your sketch."

Anne left the room and a few minutes later Uncle Wayne arrived to train with Alex, but Anne was not with him.

Alex didn't see Anne again until right before dinner. She cornered him in the front hallway. "Never enter my past again!" she hissed.

"I'm sorry. I didn't . . . ." Alex meant to embarrass, not hurt her. Seeing her memory second-hand was unbearable. For her, the pain would seem real. The thought of Anne in real danger never occurred to him. He was always Seth's target.

⚜ ⚜ ⚜ ⚜ ⚜

The Met's elevator lurched to a stop and the doors swished open, jolting Alex out of Spain and back to his present problems. Everything was different now. This time, Seth wanted Anne, not him. Anne needed a real protector — not a teasing brother.

Alex followed Selena into the Douglas Dillon Boardroom. Uncle Wayne rose from the conference room table to greet them.

"Wayne? I thought Marcus —" Selena said with concern.

"He's on his way with Anne." Wayne turned to Alex. "Your mom's strong. She'll hold on until we find her."

A girl Alex's age gracefully rose from the table to join them. Wayne stared disapprovingly at her. "Miss Chasca here took an unauthorized fieldtrip. Emma caught her wandering through the Asian Art galleries. With all the commotion, Isadora thought it safest for her to travel back to the estate with us."

"Are you a Collective student, too?" Chasca asked, flashing Alex a brilliant smile. "I'm studying the Crystal Tablet."

"What you are," Wayne insisted, "is suspended. Absolutely no off-estate portal travel for three days."

Other than his cousin George, Alex hadn't met the other students studying with the Collective. Alex wanted to say

28

something impressive, but his mind went blank. He absently ran his hand through his hair and — argh — his finger tangled in knots halfway down the back of his head. Chasca's smile vanished. Great, Alex thought. In less than a minute, I've grossed her out.

Chasca pointed at the doorway. "Marcus!"

"Lamia's here with a full team," Marcus said. He flinched as Wayne examined his head.

"Is Anne hurt?" Alex asked. "Oh my God, did Seth capture her, too?"

Marcus gently squeezed Alex's shoulder. "She's fine. You'll see her at the estate." He tried to give Alex a reassuring grin, but winced in pain before he could pull it off.

Selena glared at Marcus. "You promised me The Met was secure." Alex thought she might add to Marcus's bruises.

"It still is," he insisted. "Now, if you will follow me —"

"Are we using San Nicolo's doorway?" Chasca asked, eagerly.

"That's the plan," Marcus said. "The door is the safest portal."

Marcus led the way through galleries and down a long hallway to the Great Stairs. He stopped as he reached the top of the stairs and muttered, "Not helpful."

Alex peered over the railing. A tour group blocked the first landing. Their guide's voice boomed off the arched ceiling. He followed Marcus's gaze beyond the tourists to the bottom of the stairs. There, a blonde woman, dressed in a dark green suit, waited with several rough-looking men. The blonde saw Marcus, then glared at Alex. Even from a distance, her eyes bore into him.

Although Alex already knew the answer, he whispered, "Lamia?"

Marcus nodded.

She pointed at Alex, and her men charged up the stairs, pushing past and knocking over tourists.

Together they fled through the European Painting galleries, out onto a balcony overlooking the Arms and Armor hall and rushed through a glass door into the Musical Instruments gallery. Alex bounded past grand pianos, across another balcony and down stairs to the Arms and Armor hall. Marcus put his arm out to keep Alex from spilling into the room. He scanned the gallery, searching for Lamia's agents.

Wayne pointed to the ceiling. Given the shouts from angry tourists, their pursuers were forcing their way through the crowd.

"They're too close. We can't let them see us use the portal," Marcus said. "We'll take a more conventional exit."

"Let's try the Temple first," Wayne suggested. "We'll gain distance on the way to the Great Hall. We can lose them in the Egyptian Art galleries."

"You're prepared for Gallery 128?" Marcus asked.

"Henhenet should be in Cairo visiting the Egyptian Museum," Wayne replied.

They sped across the hall, but as Alex passed a procession of four knights on horseback, the summer day's brilliance spilled through the arched windows, splashed off the polished armor and danced across the walls. Not now! Alex thought as his world slowed down. Paralyzed, he watched a black-and-gold suit of armor burst out of its display case, jump across the room and swallow Marcus. The knight opened his visor, but Marcus's clean-shaven face wasn't inside. Instead, a man with a beard and a massive mustache stared down at Alex.

This man's life flashed through Alex's mind. A young boy became Sir George Clifford, 3rd Earl of Cumberland. Alex cringed from physical pain of countless jousting battles that earned Sir George the title of Queen Elizabeth's Champion. He experienced Sir George's joy when his sons were born and his despair when they died. The image shifted and Alex tasted salty air. Sir George was sailing aboard the *Scourge of Malice* headed to siege the El Morro castle in Puerto Rico.

Sir George grabbed Alex by the shoulders. "Intruder! Throw him overboard!"

The channel broke and Alex was back at The Met. Sir George's armor stood at attention in the display case, and Wayne was dragging Alex from the room. Lamia's men had reached the bottom of the stairs. Alex's journey with Sir George lost valuable time.

As they rushed through the medieval galleries and into the Great Hall, Alex shook his head, trying to clear his mind. Three men at the entrance pointed at them. Lamia had the main exits covered. Marcus didn't slow. They reached the Egyptian wing and disappeared into the exhibits.

"In here!" Marcus directed them into a side passageway.

"Get back here! They'll see you," Chasca hissed at Alex.

"They won't be here for another thirty-eight seconds," Alex said. He peered around the corner to catch a glimpse of their pursuers.

"How can you be sure?" she whispered, grabbing Alex's backpack to pull him deeper into the passageway.

Alex counted down. "Now." He nodded toward the gallery as Lamia's men passed.

"You're a Carnelian Tablet student," Chasca whispered in awe. "Even Wayne can't see into the future. Where are Lamia's men going?"

Alex shrugged. "I can't control when the visions come. My dreams, though, are scary accurate." He swallowed hard, thinking of the flight from Seattle to New York. He hoped to dream about Mom — to find where Seth took her. Instead, he trudged through one of his recurring nightmares — the one when he shot an innocent old woman.

"The gallery is clear. Let's move," Marcus said. "Stay close." He guided Chasca into the next gallery, but Alex stopped stone dead, shivering in the doorway.

"Welcome to Gallery 128," Wayne said.

To say ghosts gathered in this room was an understatement. Cold mist swirled in little eddies as spirits wafted around a dark stone tablet near the center of the room. Some ghosts poured buckets of opaque water over the stone, while others fought to drink the liquid dripping from the stone base.

Chasca walked through the room. Alex wanted to follow her, but too many ghosts drifted between them. He hated walking through spirits. Their pain and torment made him nauseous. "Isn't there another way?"

Wayne whispered, "They'll let you pass. They're obsessed with drinking the waters from the Magical Stela. Nectanebo II had thirteen healing spells carved on the stone. The ghosts believe the spells will save their souls, but they're meant to cure poisonings. Henhenet is the only one who can cast them properly. Come on. Keep to the side."

Alex crept behind his uncle. They were passing the Stela, when Wayne hesitated. "She's here."

A burly ghost called out. "Make way for Queen Henhenet, beloved wife of King Mentuhotep, the King's Sole Ornament and Priestess of Hathor!"

"Not anymore!" An elegant young woman in flowing linens entered the room. "How many times must I tell you? I curse Hathor!" The other ghosts cowered as she neared, and opened a path to the Stela. Henhenet ignored them. She glared at Wayne. "You dare to enter my realm?"

"What did you do to her?" Alex asked.

Wayne prodded Alex toward the exit. "I tried to help. It was a colossal mistake. She doesn't want her soul saved. She's one messed-up ghost."

Henhenet pointed at Wayne. "Possess him!"

Alex wanted to race to the exit, but the ghosts blocked his way. He skirted the edge of the room, while his Uncle Wayne stood between Alex and the Queen's guards. As they neared the door, Wayne began chanting.

Henhenet mocked Wayne, "You lack the power to summon a greater deity."

"I just need a diversion," Wayne said, grabbing Alex and yanking him out of the room.

"Shhh!" Selena turned to Alex, pressing her finger to her lips. She pointed into the glass gallery housing the temple where Lamia and her men searched the room.

Alex glanced back into Gallery 128. Wayne had summoned Heka, god of magic and medicine. His two huge snakes snapped at Henhenet. Great, Alex thought, a maniacal priestess behind us, and a cold-blooded killer in the next room.

Marcus scurried them into a side gallery. Alex and Chasca crouched behind a mummy's coffin while the adults guarded the entrance.

"Can we double back through the Egyptian Galleries?" Selena asked.

Wayne shook his head. "I wouldn't recommend it. Henhenet will be waiting for me."

"I'll create a portal," Selena offered.

Marcus backed away from her. "No, thanks. You've been out of practice for too long."

"Let's try the Frank Lloyd Wright room," Wayne suggested. "I haven't used it, but Emma claims the exit is ready."

Marcus agreed and they wove their way through the museum to the American Arts wing. No one followed them as they slipped into an exhibit closed for renovation. Marcus stepped over the rope barrier and skirted the outside edge of the deserted Frank Lloyd Wright room.

Chasca peered out the window beyond the museum's ground. "Are we going to escape into Central Park?"

"No, Lamia has the building surrounded," Marcus said. "We're leaving through an abandoned bomb shelter. It connects to a series of underground tunnels. Emma drained the floodwater last week. Watch your step. The floor may be slick."

Alex was the last to enter the shabby stairwell leading to the passage beneath The Met. As they descended, the air turned musty and water stains appeared on the walls. He grimaced, thinking of the week before the Great East Coast Flood. Mom wanted to give Anne a surprise shopping/museum trip to New York, but the night before their flight, Alex had another disturbing nightmare.

✠✠✠✠✠

In his dream, he was a woman named Antonia, living in the city of Herculaneum in 79 AD. Her neighbor, a cruel man, beat his servants daily. Early in the morning, she heard a scream. The man was brutally whipping a young girl. Welts covered her arms and legs, and blood gushed from a cut over her eyebrow.

Antonia had to do something or he might kill the child. She ran into the garden and pointed to the mountain across the bay. "You are angering Vesuvius!" Her neighbor looked wide-eyed at the fires growing on the mountain. He released the girl and ran. Antonia hurried to the girl's side.

"Take me to the water," the girl begged.

Antonia helped her down the steep path to the shore beneath the cliffs. As they reached the sea, the earth began to shake. The water slowly rose, covering their feet, and then fled, rushing away from the shore.

"Finally, my pain will end. I am exhausted," the girl lamented. "First from heaven, then to earth, this time it must be by water, in the midst of fire. My time has come." She chased the retreating sea toward the great wave. Seconds before the tsunami consumed her, the slave girl transformed into Anne.

Alex woke up, drenched in sweat. Thankfully, Mom believed his premonition — Anne will die if she goes to New York. She immediately canceled the trip to New York. For a week, Anne accused him of ruining her life, bringing up everything he ever did to upset her. She stopped complaining after an earthquake hit Greenland. When the massive ice sheet dislodged, flooding coastal cities around the globe, including New York, she apologized, promising never to doubt him again. Of course, it didn't last.

✠✠✠✠

"Kid, are you joining us?" Marcus called, bringing him out of the memory. The others were out of sight.

Anne was in New York. Was Anne about to die? Alex shook off the feeling and hurried to catch up. The stairs led to a bomb shelter connected to a wide tunnel. He gaped at the ceiling. "How far is it?"

"Nine blocks. The tunnel ends beneath the Lenox Hill Hospital," Marcus said.

Alex took a tentative step into the tunnel.

"What's wrong?" Chasca asked him.

"Can't you feel it?" He asked and hugged his arms against his chest. "All of New York City is up there . . . rock, dirt and garbage . . . broken water pipes . . . abandoned gas lines . . . and tons and tons of bugs and rats." Alex was claustrophobic. In past life number five, he was buried alive in the basement of his best friend's house. He escaped; she died.

Selena spoke quietly to Alex. "You must find the beauty in chaos. Think of New York City as a huge, shifting maze. Befriend the rats and bugs. They know their way around and the way out." Alex nodded, steeled his jaw and stepped forward.

Once they reached the hospital, Marcus led them through deserted rooms and out onto a loading dock. He hailed a taxi van and everyone piled in. "Grand Central Terminal," Marcus said to the driver.

36

The cabbie frowned at Marcus's bloodstained shirt, shrugged and sped off, weaving through the all-taxi traffic.

At the station, Marcus flashed the terminal guard his credentials and, despite his ragged condition, the guard opened the gate. After a thirty-story elevator ride, they were standing on an aerotrain platform.

Marcus pulled his comm-pad from his jeans pocket and shook it a few times. "Lamia damaged more than my head. The screen's shot, but I should be able to contact the estate." He stepped a few paces away to make the call. "Abigail, I need you at Grand Central . . . . Sorry . . . the details can wait. Get here — fast."

Wayne pulled Alex aside. "You channeled someone when we were in the Arms and Armory hall, didn't you?"

"A piece of armor swallowed Marcus, and he became Sir George Clifford," Alex said.

"My favorite armor in the exhibit," Marcus said as his face lightened into a huge grin. "Sir George Clifford and me — your talents are improving."

Wayne whispered to Alex, "He really was Sir Clifford. I've been through Marcus's past lives." Seeing Alex's confused expression, Wayne added, "Isadora insists the Collective leaders open their past lives. She keeps hoping one life will reveal the secrets of the Carnelian Tablet."

"Marcus, who beat the crap out of you this time?" a woman said from behind them.

Marcus straightened up and frowned at the woman. "Abigail, what took you so long?"

"Wow! You look bad," Abigail said, ignoring Marcus's sour

mood. After giving Selena a quick hug, she led them around the safety gate barring the platform edge.

"Are you ready?" Abigail asked Chasca, who answered with a broad smile. "Enjoy it. After this, you're grounded."

Alex peered over the edge. The thirty-story drop made him dizzy and he retreated a few steps.

"I hear the train. Come on. We must jump before it arrives."

"Jump?" Alex gasped in disbelief as Chasca grabbed his arm and pulled him over the platform's edge.

Chapter Five

Grandpa's Crazy Keys

The cushy chair gave Anne little comfort as Grandmother swished her finger across a comm-pad. Anne could no longer sit still. She stood and crossed to one of the bookcases. Bronze elephants, leopards, tigers and ostriches paraded on the shelf in front of colorful leather-bound books toward a grapefruit-sized silver ball covered with metallic ants. Anne scrunched her nose at the ants, choosing instead to touch a leopard.

"I wouldn't," Isadora said without looking up.

The leopard swiped at Anne's little finger. She yanked her hand away and gently sucked the papercut-like scratch.

"You should do something productive while we wait for Alex. You might find one of those books interesting," Isadora suggested, pointing to another bookcase.

After making sure the shelf was animal-free, Anne glanced over the titles and settled on *Inside Bruegel: The Kaleidoscope of Children's Games*. Her legs tingled as her hand neared the book. She stumbled through the bookcase into a narrow hallway.

"You must detect a portal faster or you will injure yourself," Isadora warned and slid past Anne to open a normal-looking door. Bright light flooded into the dim hall. The adjoining room, a massive arcade with one-way glass, provided panoramic views of a mountain forest and a lake.

"Are we really in New Jersey?" Anne asked. When she thought of New Jersey, she pictured cities and sprawling suburbs.

"We keep the estate's exact location private. We've camouflaged the entire complex. Even those who arrive by air see a forest dotted by a few cabins and an old farm."

Isadora walked toward the interior wall where restoration supplies and equipment flanked piles of tapestries, sculptures and paintings. An old man stared out of his portrait at Anne, his eyes following her as she walked. She shuddered and quickly joined Isadora who was inspecting a huge, unframed canvas.

"Hey, you painted a selfie," Anne said. Isadora's self-portrait exuded confidence and determination, head held high, jaw set and eyes glowing with pride. The same way she beamed when she spoke about Alex's abilities — unlike the frowns and forced smiles she reserved for Anne.

Isadora pulled a cloth over her portrait. "This version of me is not ready for visitors. We have time to take the scenic route to my meditation room while Abigail retrieves Alex."

Anne had met Aunt Abigail only once.

Three years ago, Abigail arrived, unannounced, in the middle of their living room searching for George (Anne's cousin). George's talents emerged early. He tried to control them but usually failed, making him an even bigger family disappointment than Anne was. When he accidently created a blizzard in his room, Isadora forbade him from practicing the more complex Agate Tablet skills until he mastered the basics. A week later, George started taking D.E.Ds — Ditch the Estate Days.

"Tell George his mother is here," Mom said. Even though she was shopping when George arrived, somehow Mom knew he picked their house for his break this time.

Abigail complained to Mom. "George doesn't focus. He could be such a success. You're lucky Alex is developing well. How do you manage it?"

"Maybe, George needs more time. Ease off him a bit," Mom suggested.

"He needs discipline, not a break. He's become lazy. I want the best for George — and he needs to give me his best."

With a mom like Abigail, Anne understood why George wanted to escape. She hurried to her room and crawled out her bedroom window to join George on the roof. "Your mom's here,"

George's eyes opened wide. "Not Dad?"

Anne shook her head. "Not this time."

George huffed, "I'm surprised she noticed I was gone. She's always zipping around on Collective business."

Anne's mom called from the window. "Come inside and help with dinner. George, you may stay the night, but you must go back for your Agate Tablet lessons in the morning."

Now that Anne's talents were emerging, would her training be intense? Would she master the Crystal Tablet skills, or fizzle out — like George? She wasn't sure which would be worse. She joined Isadora who waited impatiently in front of an ornate tapestry. Isadora tugged a tassel and the tapestry withdrew into the ceiling revealing a stone slab twice Anne's height. Hieroglyphics surrounded a painting of a man with the head of a bird and a long, slender beak curving downwards. With one hand, he held a metal rod before him and, with the other he grasped a golden cross with a curved handle.

"Thoth," Anne said, recognizing the god of knowledge and magic from the illustrations surrounding the ancient Egypt crazy key poem.

"I see Alex's lessons weren't completely lost on you. This is one entrance to the Amber Tablet wing. Go ahead give his ankh a push. His key to life is the key to this door."

As Anne pressed the golden cross, the stone shifted and fresh air like a summer's breeze brushed her face. Forest green light rose from the steps and, below, Anne thought she heard leaves rustling in the wind. They descended the stairs and entered a broad, arched hall, decorated to resemble an acacia tree. Leaves covering the wall and ceiling made up the crown of the tree. A floor of smooth, brown stone slabs, stretched down the bark-lined hall to dark, mossy roots and another Thoth stone door.

"Each tablet aligns with one of the five elements. Amber is earth. From earth the tree of life grows," Isadora said as she walked down the hall toward the center of the building.

"What about the Crystal Tablet?"

"The Transcender tablet aligns with the metal element. You walked through the Crystal Epi-Olmec hall when you arrived," Isadora replied.

A spark glowing in the red-brown tree bark caught Anne's eye. She stooped to take a closer look. Wedged inside a fissure in the bark, a bottle-cap-sized gemstone spider hid.

"Don't touch them," Isadora warned, "They're fragile."

Anne quickly drew her hand away from the bark and hurried to catch up to Isadora who waited in the deep shadows of the tree roots. Slightly out of breath, Anne inhaled deeply. The air smelled earthy, like a forest in springtime. Isadora pushed Thoth's ankh and the stone door opened into a round room. Heavy brocade curtains, draped on the walls, rippled as the breeze from the Amber hall reached them.

"This is my meditation room," Isadora said reverently. "I come here to reflect on the past, and contemplate the future. Although many pass through this room, few learn its secrets. I expect you and Alex to know this room as I know it." She raised her arms and the curtains opened, revealing walls and walls of paintings rising four stories.

"There must be hundreds," Anne guessed.

"Three-thousand, nine-hundred and seven. Let me introduce you to a few," she said, pointing to a painting.

Anne immediately recognized the portrait. "Grandpa." She smiled and then turned away sadly. She still missed him.

"Hubert is a brilliant man," Isadora said, beaming at the painting.

Anne frowned. Did Isadora say "is" instead of "was?"

Isadora's gaze lingered on Hubert's portrait. "He wrote *Grandpa's Crazy Keys* for you. Even though you didn't demonstrate tablet talents, he claimed you deserved training. He was right, as usual."

"Mom wanted Dad to teach me to use the Crazy Keys."

Isadora looked startled. "When did she speak with your father?"

Anne stared at her hands, wishing she could have spoken with him. "It was in a letter she wrote him before I was born."

"Those are the real keys," Isadora said, pointing to the narrow table under Grandpa's portrait. On a purple velvet stand, lay a bracelet. Five golden keys hung at even intervals on the delicate armor chain.

Isadora draped the bracelet over her fingers. "Once, I believed these keys would open doors to wondrous places, but they don't even bend time. Your father and Gerald, Hubert's assistant, formed some crazy theories involving the keys, but their experiments failed." She placed the bracelet back on its stand.

"Then what do the keys do?" Anne asked.

"Open the doors in this complex, in a figurative sense," Isadora answered, but waved away the notion. "Do you remember the first sonnet in Grandpa's book?"

Anne knew the poems in the book by heart. She quickly ran through the lines until she reached the right part.

"If you are stuck behind my doors and find your way is lost, then spot my little sign. The pictures 'round the poems keep in mind. What's in each room and in my book align. Like pushing Thoth's ankh," Anne said, her curiosity growing. "What's behind the doors?"

Isadora laughed. "Anything you can imagine! SANDY," Isadora called looking toward the ceiling.

"Yes, Isadora," a voice replied.

44

"Please grant Anne Clarke full access to the estate," Isadora requested.

"The entire estate? Is that wise?" SANDY asked.

"Full access," Isadora insisted smiling at Anne the way she usually smiled at Alex. "I have nothing to hide from her." Isadora placed her hand on Anne's shoulder.

Anne longed for Isadora's praise, but now that her kind words finally came, Anne wasn't sure what to say.

Isadora nodded to the painting next to Grandpa's portrait. "Meet Margaret Brunel. She is your great-great-aunt. She is a character — no children of her own but generous to me when I was young."

Grandmother said 'is' instead of 'was' again, Anne realized and leaned away from Isadora.

Isadora rattled on. "She inspired me to become an artist and taught me about the Collective's mission. Her grandmother, Lady Anne Brunel, founded the Collective. She's over there."

Anne approached the picture of the attractive, older woman posing in front of a wall of paintings. "Was she an artist, too?" she asked, emphasizing the word 'was,' but Isadora didn't seem to notice.

"First and foremost she's an adventurer, but with an artistic flair. Her paintings capture the excitement of the moment. Jules Sébastien César Dumont d'Urville's explorations are her best works. *Surviving the Surge* is the one right behind Lady Brunel."

Anne stepped closer to examine the tiny painting of a three-mast sailboat nearly capsizing beneath a huge wave.

"Dumont was aboard the *Chevrette*, the boat in the painting.

During his travels, he heard that a villager had discovered a marble statue and a stone tablet on the Greek island of Milos. Dumont convinced the ship's commander to delay their departure while he bargained for the treasures. Although his funds were insufficient to acquire the statue, he bought the tablet and placed it in the ship's hold. Unfortunately, the expedition encountered stormy seas. The painting commemorates the day the Carnelian Tablet was damaged."

A playful smile danced across Isadora's face as she focused Anne's attention on twelve neatly-framed drawings hung in a column.

"Those are mine!"

"Yes, each year I framed your best work. While you're here, I can help you hone your skills," Isadora promised. "Although your sketches and paintings are technically solid, they still lack depth. You must learn to capture the essence of your subject and help them decide how to improve their world. Until then, no matter how good your composition, your art will remain commonplace."

Anne lowered her head. She was accustomed to Isadora's blunt criticism, but it still stung.

"Stop pouting," Isadora scolded. "Let's start with something simple." She pointed at a picture Anne drew when she was three. "Fix your eyes on the drawing. Focus on the colors and texture of the crayon, the fabric of the paper. Pick a distinctive feature and imagine yourself as part of the scene." Isadora clutched Anne's hand and they disappeared from the meditation room.

Anne landed inside the crayon drawing. She backed away from the huge strands of blue ribbon outlining the house.

46

"Grandmother, where are you?" she asked, staggering past the gray cat and down the front steps into the white nothingness of paper. "How do I get out of here? What if I can't leave?" As Anne panicked, Isadora popped into the drawing.

"Sorry, I took a little trip into the past. Calm down. Portal Protocol #1 —"

"I know. Panicky portals produce pandemonium. Bixia already lectured me."

"Take my hand and we'll go." They landed back in the meditation room. Isadora leaned toward Anne and winked. "I hope we didn't give anyone nightmares. People near the painting can sometimes hear you."

"Don't worry," Bixia said, startling Anne. She rose from the table to join them. "I was frightened the first time I got stuck in a painting. It happens to everyone."

Bixia must have arrived while they were in the drawing, Anne realized, and wondered how long they were away. Then it struck her. What if I'm stranded in a painting — forever? "How did we leave the drawing?" she asked.

"Isadora pictured her meditation room," Bixia said.

"That's it?"

"Can you describe, in detail, any part of this room?" Isadora asked.

Anne shook her head.

Isadora gave her a curt nod. "I didn't think so. Until you learn to sift time, you require a tether — a visual link to where you begin a journey."

"Can I move in time?" Anne asked, questions flooding into her mind.

"It will take some practice before you manage to travel safely. Once you master the basics, though, you may visit the places the painting has hung. I looked in on your mother while we were inside your crayon drawing. She was making dinner for you and Alex."

"You saw Mom?" Anne stared at her drawing, desperate to jump back inside. "Is it hard to do?"

"Hopping through paintings is easy compared to navigating your portal," Bixia laughed.

"Do you understand what happened inside Anne's mess?" Isadora asked.

Bixia touched icons on her data pad and showed it to Isadora. "Lamia managed to detect Anne's portal signature, she even manipulated it."

"She wanted me to jump through the blue light," Anne said, gently pressed her fingertips, still red and tender from burning them.

Isadora exclaimed, "Lamia created an exit?"

"We better shut down the older portals. If Lamia cracks one, we risk a full breach."

"Why won't Seth's agents leave us alone?" Anne asked.

Isadora took a deep breath and turned to Grandpa's portrait, contemplating the idea for a few moments before answering Anne. "Seth is a twisted, power-hungry fiend. He steals from brilliant scientists and pushes their ideas to the extreme without stopping to understand the chaos he might cause. He has no ethics or regard for human life —" Isadora's voice cracked.

Bixia gently placed her hand on Isadora's arm and explained,

"Seth is obsessed with time dimensions. When he abducted Hubert, Seth tried to 'extract' our secrets from him. Hubert resisted. Seth didn't give up. He has tried — unsuccessfully — to use technology to travel across time. Each time he fails, the side effects magnify, causing destructive earthquakes and tsunamis."

"If he succeeds, he could unleash unimaginable forces on Earth," Isadora said. Her expression softened. "Thankfully, most of Hubert's knowledge, and much of what he felt, I imprinted on this canvas before Seth killed him. Hubert's life remains intact. His simulated world allows him to spend time with me and help train future members of the Collective."

Anne looked up at the wall. "You mean he is alive, and the other paintings, too?"

"Oh, no, no, but that would be fun, wouldn't it?" Isadora glanced back at Grandpa's painting. "Without my abilities, all that Hubert was would have disappeared."

"What does he do in there? Is he lonely?" Anne asked. "Can you imagine life trapped in a painting?"

"He's happy!" Isadora declared emphatically. She stiffened, then pressed the smile back on her face. "He lives in a lovely, elaborate biosimulation with his memories packaged up and stored on the canvas."

Bixia's data pad chimed. "I hate to break up this cozy lesson, but Marcus and Alex are leaving New York City. Anne, do you mind waiting here? SANDY can let them know where you are. Isadora and I should finish analyzing your portal."

Anne shrugged slightly, a fresh wave of guilt hitting her. Her portal had caused so much trouble and now Seth might have learned enough from it to infiltrate the estate. She walked aimlessly around the room, until she found herself back at Grandpa's painting.

"You're not real," she told him, "but I wish you were." She reached for the Crazy Key bracelet and slipped it on her wrist. Voices exploded in her mind. The paintings awakened, alive with whirling faces and windows to strange rooms. Grandpa's face melted, morphing into an ugly bat-like beast. Its charcoal body and wings sizzled with white lightning, and its mouth, eyes, and tail glowed blood-red.

Anne ran to the Thoth door and yanked on his ankh. She shoved until it closed, and leaned against the slab. In the deep shadows of the tree roots, she listened for the beast. The tree trembled, as if a strong breeze threatened to break its branches. The winged monster has followed me, Anne thought. Glowing mist wafted from the gnarled roots, as tiny sparks flickered in the bark along the hall. Sap oozed from the tree as worms, spiders, and ants awoke. Anne gasped and raced for the far end of the hall, where light bounced off the green leaves framing a stairway — her escape!

More bugs and grubs sprang to life as she ran passed them. When she reached the upper branches, the inviting woodland-green light turned jaundice. From above, she heard a single chirp. Three more chirps answered. A loud buzzing ricocheted down the stairs and off the leaves, as hundreds of jeweled hummingbirds swarmed around her. They were deafening! She pressed her back against the tree branches, arms protecting her face. A hummingbird pecked at her hand with its amber beak. She knew if she didn't escape, they would overwhelm her and the beast would catch her. She dropped to her knees still swatting tiny birds, but too many darted around her head. A mass of gemstone creatures skittered toward her along the tree trunk. Within seconds, the horde arrived. Her back now covered in creatures, she leaned against the tree trunk trying to squish them. A section of the wall gave way, dropping her into a dark room.

Anne rolled off the broken bug pieces. Her left hip and ankle hurt. Bruised — not broken she decided. Hummingbirds continued to swarm through the square opening she had fallen through. She called for help, but her voice didn't carry far and no one responded. Taking short, shuffling steps, her arms outstretched to feel for obstacles, she searched for a wall. As she moved farther and farther from the square of light and the hummingbirds, a cold draft wafted around her ankles. Still shuffling, she shifted her right foot forward. It dipped down where the floor dropped away. A faint clicking sound, reminding her of the scurrying gemstone spiders, came from below. She hoped the pit was deep and there was no way for whatever made the clicking sound to escape. As she backed away from the pit, the light faded as the square opening closed.

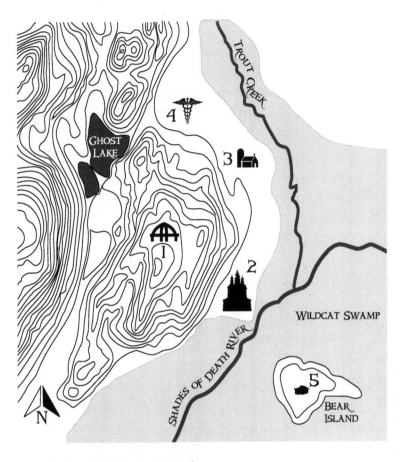

The Collective's Estate:
1. Tablet Complex
2. Isadora's Home
3. Uncle Thomas's Farm
4. Aunt Helena's Medical Center
5. George's Shack

CHAPTER SIX

THE ESTATE

Alex screamed and clutched Chasca's arm as they fell. She whooped — her arms spread wide — as the ground neared. The air crackled, then split; Alex jolted to a stop.

"Let go," Chasca complained, prying his fingers off her arm.

"Transportation Alert: New arrivals in the transportation center," a voice said.

Selena glared at a camera on the ceiling. "I hate that security system."

"My name is SANDY and hate is a very strong word," the security system scolded.

Still struggling to catch his breath, Alex stared at the glowing, red camera light.

"Alex is distressed," SANDY reported. "Do you require medical attention?"

Marcus clapped Alex on the back. "He's fine. Right?"

Alex tried to appear confident but managed only a weak smile. Arriving at the estate was supposed to be the turning point in his life, but he wasn't an Amalgamator, not yet, his training was incomplete. Anne's portal accident brought him here before he was ready. Worry and guilt robbed him of the excitement he was expecting. He had to find Anne and, somehow, help Mom. Still weak and wobbly from the jump, he got to his feet slowly.

Chasca stared at him with either concern or disgust — he wasn't sure which. She tilted her head as if puzzled. "I guess I'll see you around the estate," she said, following Abigail out of the room.

Alex watched her skip down a silvery hall until she disappeared from view.

"SANDY, where is Isadora," Marcus asked.

"Art Studio, Amber Section." SANDY replied.

Marcus guided Alex into a hallway supported by limestone columns. Gold hieroglyphics covered the walls.

"Fantastic, isn't it?" Marcus said. "The room is a replica of the temple where the Amber Tablet was discovered."

More like a tomb, Alex thought.

"Do you know which part of the complex we're in?" Marcus asked.

"Amber wing on the transportation level," Alex answered absently, not caring if he were right.

"Good and how many levels?" Marcus continued the quiz.

"Seven."

They stopped midway up the hall and Selena placed her hand over a symbol on the wall. A door opened into a square, paneled room. When the door swept shut, the whole room lurched and started rising.

"Want to guess which way is out?" Marcus asked Alex.

"Marcus, please. Timing is critical in here," Selena said.

Ignoring Selena's objections, Marcus continued Alex's lesson. "Your mom grew up in this wing of the complex. If you inherited some of her Amber Tablet abilities, spending time in these passageways might —"

SANDY, interrupting Marcus, began to count down, "Thirty-five, thirty-four, thirty-three . . ."

"What's SANDY doing?" Alex asked.

Selena looked at her watch before replying. "You have twenty-seven seconds left to find the door and key before SANDY locks us in the elevator. Then we wait until Isadora or one of the other masters releases us."

Alex groaned. Spouting out Tablet Complex facts was easy. He knew the layout of the building; memorizing it when he was ten. The last thing he needed right now was a stressful, timed test. He quickly scanned the room. Three walls were smooth, but a scene inlaid in wood dominated the center of the fourth. Two robed men, arms held high, worshiped a tree. Its branches rose through the clouds to heaven.

"Seventeen, sixteen, fifteen . . ."

Alex focused on the stars, planets, and moons growing like fruit from the branches. Nothing looked promising. Birds and insects perched in circles outlining the tree. He slid his finger down the trunk and found two tiny symbols hidden among its knotted roots — Maat's ostrich feather and Thoth's moon disc.

"Go ahead. Give his disc a push," Selena urged.

Alex touched it with one finger. It shifted, and the adjacent wall panel slid into the floor.

"Two seconds to spare. Congratulations," SANDY cheered. "Your mother caused three lockdowns before she figured it out."

Alex drew a calming breath. "I like secret doors and hidden passageways as much as anyone, but are all the doors in the complex like this?"

Selena gently touched the roots, carefully avoiding the moon disc. "Dad created these crazy doors to keep us on our toes when we were kids. He loved challenging puzzles and a good joke." She added with disgust, "He also programmed SANDY to tattle on us."

"I protect you," SANDY corrected.

Selena rolled her eyes as she led Alex into what looked like a mad scientist's laboratory. Colorful liquids in strange glass vessels cluttered the workbenches. Collection hoods, hanging from the ceiling, sucked up foul gases emitted from vats of oozing, greasy slime. A domed fireplace, centered in the floor, heated an iron cauldron. Alex peeked into the pot. Dark brown, frothy sludge churned as it boiled. A little geyser of gunk erupted and smacked Alex's cheek.

"Stay clear of the apparatus," Marcus warned. "That stuff can melt your skin."

Alex wiped his face with his shirtsleeve and retreated to the edge of the room.

"I'd be more afraid of Isadora's wrath. She spends months

perfecting her alchemy experiments," Selena said, pulling open a little cabinet. She fiddled with numbered squares in a grid. As she pushed the last number into place, a door opened. Soothing green light flooded the room.

"You will love this hall," Marcus promised. "It's filled with brilliant green leaves, cute critters hiding in the tree and —"

"Stop!" Selena yelled, as they stepped into the hall. Little jeweled bird and insect statues littered the floor. "Don't move. You might hurt them. They take years to create."

"Where did they come from?" Alex asked.

"The tree bark, but I don't know how they escaped," Selena said, as she gently sorted the delicate creatures into piles.

"What caused them to animate? Even if we crammed all our Level Seven Amber into this hall, they couldn't awaken this many creatures," Marcus said.

Alex followed Selena as she cleared a path. They reached a set of stairs where little hummingbirds, some with broken beaks, others missing wings, lay strewn in a pile. Something or someone had slaughtered them. At the top of the steps, Selena opened a Thoth-shaped door. They found Isadora and Bixia in a kitchenette reserved for art renovation specialists.

Bixia winced at the sight of Marcus. "Abigail told me you were a mess, but you've outdone yourself this time —"

Marcus interrupted. "We had a massive transfiguration event on the meditation level."

"I left Anne in the meditation room. SANDY, where is Anne?" Isadora demanded.

"Anne is in the Simulation Containment Vessel E2 between the meditation and research levels," SANDY reported.

"The air duct? How'd she get down there?" Marcus asked. "The simulation is sealed."

"Isadora gave Anne full access," SANDY replied. "If she remains in the Vessel during the hatch she will contaminate the environment and ruin the results."

"Hatch? When?" Selena asked.

"In eight minutes and twenty-three seconds the temperature will increase from sub-freezing to one-hundred degrees Fahrenheit. Shall I provide a count down?" SANDY asked.

"No!" Selena and Bixia said together.

Bixia opened a Tablet Complex map on her data pad. "There. She's near the edge of the breeding habitat."

Alex stared at the blip marking Anne's location. "What type of experiment are you running?"

"Agate insect management tests," Marcus replied. "We have to extract her before the insects emerge."

The thought of climbing into an air duct to help Anne made Alex's stomach tighten. He knew one of his past lives caused his claustrophobia, but knowing that didn't help him control it. Cramped quarters didn't faze Anne, but things flying around her head did — even butterflies creeped her out. For Anne's sake, Alex hoped the insects were the crawling type and kept their legs on the ground.

Chapter Seven

Experimenting with Agates

Anne ran her hands along the smooth metal wall, searching for a door. The wall was endless. She pounded it with her fists and yelled for help. Frustrated, she sank to the floor and hugged her knees to her chest. At least the humming birds were roosting. She stared into the darkness toward the pit and shivered, not from the cold draft emitting from it, but the mechanical sounds deep inside it. When she fell into the room, clicks came only once or twice a second. Now, whirring sounds replaced the clicking and the pit began to glow.

She crawled to the edge and peered inside — hoping to find it empty. At its base, a faint light, like dawn, streaked a cement floor with blues and purples. The light intensified into reddish-greens, pinks. The cool draft warmed and the shadows in the shaft receded enough for Anne to see a ladder bolted to the wall. She retreated from the pit to consider her options. In a burst of light, the pit radiated bright yellow beams lighting the entire room. Above her, she saw the hatch she had fallen through. A ladder, covered with sleeping humming birds, extended above it connecting to another hatch near an exhaust fan. There was no way to reach it. The only way out was down.

Squinting to shield her eyes from the bright light, Anne dangled her legs near the ladder until she found a foothold. Carefully easing her body over the edge, she grabbed the top rung. The once cool draft strengthened into a strong hot breeze blowing her hair into the air. By the time she reached the bottom rung, sweat dripped down her face. Anne quickly scanned the room. Walls made of fine mesh surrounded a ten-foot square concrete slab. There was a screen door in one of the walls but, outside, the air was thick with flies, wasps, stinkbugs and mosquitos buzzing around in a garden larger than a gymnasium. In the center of the garden, Anne saw the source of the mechanical whirring. Numbers on a neon billboard spun, counting the insect population — now nearing 53 million. A second billboard flickered to life, "Praying Mantis Population," and began clicking.

As the temperature and humidity continued to climb, the mosquitos, looking for a blood-snack, coated the mesh walls, trying to reach Anne. Would the mesh hold up? She decided she wouldn't stick around to find out. As Anne neared the top of the ladder, a green triangular head, attached to a long neck, peered over the edge. The praying mantis rocked its head back and forth but kept its compound eyes on Anne. It crept over the edge and inched toward her.

"You won't hurt me — right?" she asked the insect as long as her hand. It crawled onto Anne's arm, sped to the top of her head and paused. The mantis's legs move through her hair. Anne squeezed her eyes shut; her entire body tensed. "Please don't tangle," she begged. The mantis climbed down Anne's other arm and scooted down the ladder.

Above her, mantis heads surrounded the rim of the pit. She retreated to the screened-in room where the first mantis clawed the wall near the door. Beyond it, the mantis counter spun past five thousand. Across the garden, a cloud of insects rolled like a storm front toward Anne. Mantises poured down on her and marched toward the screen. She pulled her shirt over her mouth, covered her ears with her hands and closed her eyes tightly.

The screen door flapped open. Anne pressed her elbows to her sides and held her breath.

"Hurry up, Simon. I can't do this forever." Marcus said.

Anne cautiously opened one eye. Standing in the doorway was a black-haired, teenaged boy with bright blue eyes. Behind him Marcus stood, hands raised to the sky, holding the insect horde at bay. As the mantises poured into the garden, the boy reached his hand out to help Anne to her feet. She hesitated as he led her toward the door.

"I'll shield you," Simon said as he pulled her close. "Marcus will clear the way and I can keep the insects away, but move quickly. The tiger mosquitos are hungry and won't listen to my suggestions for much longer."

Anne allowed Simon to lead her out of the mesh shelter into

the swarm. Most of the insects stayed at arm's length, but a few mosquitos buzzed in and out of Simon's protective bubble. Anne stared at the ground as they walked through the garden, occasionally seeing a praying mantis strike, capturing an insect in its powerful arms. When they reached the exit, Marcus created a path and Simon and Anne scooted through the door. Despite Marcus's efforts, thousands of mosquitos followed them into the decontamination room. Anne held tightly to Simon as he tried his best to shield her, but the mosquitos buzzed and bit, no longer willing to forgo their feast.

"Stand in the center of the room," Marcus yelled as he slapped a red button on the wall.

The door sealed and a cold breeze swirled around their bodies, fluffing their clothing and hair and blowing the insects toward the wall where they died in a cacophony of pops and zaps. As the smell of charred bugs and electricity faded, a door opened. Alex, looking anxious, stood between Selena and Isadora. Although Anne wanted to rush to Alex, she didn't want to leave Simon. When she was near him, her sadness seemed to evaporate. For the first time since she left Collinsville, she felt reassured and comforted.

She turned to thank him, but before she could, he said, "No worries. Insect management is kind of my thing."

Marcus placed his hand on Simon's shoulder. "Well done, now go figure out how much Anne messed up our experiment. When you're done, meet me in the Agate Tablet wing. I'd say you've graduated from bugs. Reptiles are up next."

Anne's confidence drained as Simon sidestepped Alex and disappeared from view.

Selena gathered Anne in a hug. "Are you okay?"

Anne pulled away from her. "No! First Mom . . . then this thing in the meditation room — it was horrible."

"Anne, dear, pull yourself together," Isadora said impatiently. "Whatever you think happened, I'm sure I can fix it."

Anne tried to stiffen up. "I wanted to see how the bracelet would look on me. So I tried it on. I wasn't going to take it or anything. A huge monster —" She brushed at her wrist as if trying to clean away an army of ants. The bracelet fell to the floor.

"Monster?" Isadora dismissed the idea. "Your trip into the drawing messed up your internal clock. Hallucinations are common with time lag."

Was it all in her mind? No, not all of it, she decided. "I know I didn't imagine the hummingbirds." She raised her hand, showing where the bird pecked her.

"You were there when they animated?" Isadora asked, her eyes gleaming. "Let's go to the Amber hall and see what happens. I promise I won't let anything harm you."

Anne knew Isadora couldn't keep that promise. "Can't it wait?" she pleaded.

"Isadora! Stop obsessing! Anne needs rest and time to absorb what has happened," Selena said.

"All right, take the kids to the house and get them settled," Isadora agreed as she picked up the bracelet. "Aunt Margaret will get to the bottom of this in the morning."

Anne mindlessly followed Selena through the maze of halls and out of the building. It wasn't until they reached the end of the stone path sloping into the woods, that she noticed Alex was shouldering two backpacks. "You saved my stuff!"

Alex slid the bag off and held it out to her. Anne grabbed it and unzipped the main pocket. "You even packed my journals and Fosby!" Anne pulled her favorite stuffed bear to her chest. Although she wanted to contain them, tears flowed down her cheek. She felt frail and broken. She sniffed, wiped away her tears and gently placed Fosby into the backpack. She looked up at Alex gratefully. Although he tried to look confident, Anne saw his exhaustion and sadness. The last twenty-four hours were rough on him, too, she realized. "I'll carry my pack," she said, not wanting to burden him more.

Selena led them down a path overgrown with prickly bushes. After a few hundred feet, the path opened to a vast swamp. "Welcome to Wild Cat Swamp. The Shades of Death River flows through the middle of it. Some say the river got its name because mountain lions killed many of the settlers. Others blame the mosquitoes. In 1850, there was a horrible malaria outbreak. They drained the swamp in the late 1800s, but, as you can see, it returned. What do you think, Alex? Death is your specialty."

Alex stared at the mounds of swamp grass. Anne knew the river spooked him and, if it spooked Alex, she knew to avoid it and stayed close to Selena. As the path curved, the forest and swampland gave way to grassy fields where a long, gravel driveway wound to an enormous mansion. Wide marble steps, bordered by flower gardens, rose to an ornate gate sparkling in the muted sunlight.

"That's Isadora's house?" Alex exclaimed.

"Yes, I grew up here," Selena said, "Members of the Collective and students also stay here when they visit the estate.

As they reached the top of the marble steps, the gates opened into a courtyard where a fountain spouted. Behind it, five towers cast dark shadows across the courtyard.

"Unending," Anne said.

Selena grinned. "The mansion is difficult to take in with one glance, but it does have an end. Wait until you see the inside."

Anne stepped through the front door. A gray-and-white marble floor spanned an enormous reception hall ending at a wall of windows. Second- and third-floor balconies, supported by marble colonnades, surrounded the room. Four sets of stone steps circled to the upper floors, their silver banisters reflecting light around the room.

"Maybe unending is the right description," Alex said. "This place is huge."

"The room can accommodate over five hundred people," Selena said, guiding them up the closest set of steps to a long, shadowy hallway with a single door. "That's Isadora's suite."

"Are all the rooms like this?" Anne asked, wondering why Isadora would choose to live in such a depressing part of the mansion.

"No," Selena answered. "Isadora gave us kids the upper floors. For the most part, she let us decorate our rooms the way we wanted. Anne, you may stay in your mom's room and I'm sure Isadora would want Alex to have Wayne's."

They continued circling up the steps until they reached a bright room with a balcony overlooking the entrance hall, four-stories beneath them. Even from this height, the room seemed massive.

Selena pointed to the three-story, stone tower extending through the glass ceiling. "That's your mom's room. Wayne's room is over there." She nodded toward one of the smaller towers occupying the four corners of the hall. "His faces the south, Thomas has east, mine is west and Helena has north."

"Do you still use the rooms?" Anne asked, suppressing a shudder. Helena, the youngest and deadliest of Isadora's five children, gave Anne the creeps. An Onyx Tablet master, Helena could blend into the background like a chameleon. Her medicinal tonics could heal or instantly kill.

"We moved out years ago."

Anne and Alex approached their mom's bedroom door, but neither reached for the handle.

"It shouldn't be locked," Selena said, opening the door for them.

Mom rarely spoke about her childhood or the estate. Anne wasn't sure what to expect inside the room, but the canopy bed draped in amber sheers didn't seem like something Mom would choose — neither did the fluffy, faux fur rug.

"What's up here?" Alex asked, climbing the first few steps coiling around the wall.

"Elizabeth's laboratory. You may explore later," Selena said. She opened a leather bag and handed Anne six books. "These are some of your father's journals. He was a great Transcender. I'm sure he would want you to have them."

Anne placed the journals, her only connection to her father, on the bed. "Hey, one of the journals is missing — *Responsible Art: Avoiding Deadly Results*."

"I'm sorry. It wasn't in the safe-room," Selena replied. "But I did find this." She held out Anne's copy of *Grandpa's Crazy Keys*.

Anne groaned. *If I had left that box alone, Mom would be safe.*

"Someone's coming," Alex said, interrupting her thoughts. She recognized his empty stare. He was seeing into the future. "It's bad news," he whispered.

A few seconds later, Marcus arrived looking weary and concerned. "Selena, Isadora needs you back in the Tablet Complex. Seth made his demands."

"What does he want?" Selena asked.

Marcus didn't answer and looked at Alex.

"The Primal Key?" Alex asked. Alex's face paled. "But I don't know where is it," Alex said more to himself than the others in the room. "It might take me years to connect the tablets and find the Primal Key — if it even exists."

"Elizabeth doesn't have that long," Marcus said. "Isadora thinks Seth broke Elizabeth's will. If he knows about the tablets and the Key —"

"Elizabeth wouldn't betray the Collective," Selena insisted. "She would die before giving into Seth."

"She can't die!" Anne exclaimed. She couldn't imagine Mom dying — leaving her and Alex alone — to keep some relic away from Seth.

"Why does he want this Key?" Alex asked.

"The Crystal Tablet suggests a possible link to the parallel dimensions of the Plexus," Selena answered.

Marcus placed a steadying hand on Alex's shoulder. "If we don't give the Key to Seth, he promised the earthquake that caused the Great East Coast Flood would pale in comparison to what he has planned for his next experiment —"

"And Mom?" Alex asked.

"He said Elizabeth would be at the heart of the disaster."

"We have to find it!" Anne exclaimed.

"We can't bank on connecting the tablets in time," Marcus said firmly. "I'll coordinate the attack on Seth Industries."

"He might . . . he might hurt Mom if you attack!" Anne couldn't bear to say what she feared. Seth would kill Mom if she became a liability.

"I will do everything I can to save her," Marcus promised.

"Anne, you should rest. Time lag can play tricks in your mind. I'll wake you for dinner," Selena said, closing the door as she and Marcus left.

Rest? The last thing Anne wanted to do was rest. "What do we do first? How can I help you find the missing tablet pieces and the Key?"

"Connecting the tablets is my job. You don't know anything about it," Alex said, picking up a journal. "I guess you'll want to read this one now that Isadora is going to start your training." He handed Anne a book entitled Mastering the Crystal Tablet: The Art of Transcending. "I need time alone to think. Try to stay out of trouble. I'll see you at dinner."

Anne kicked the bedpost. He always treated her like a little sister, not his twin. He was the talented one and she grew up in his shadow. No more, she told herself. If Alex couldn't find the Key, she would figure out another way to save Mom. She ran her finger along the journal's spine. "Dad, I wish you were here. You would know what to do." Wanting to feel closer to him, she opened The Art of Transcending.

Chapter Eight

ᴴᴵᴱ ᴴᴵᴱ

Alex's Steamy Bat

Uncle Wayne's room was round like Mom's, but smaller. Still, it was at least five times bigger than Alex's room in Collinsville. As he pulled his dad's jacket from his backpack, the silver ball Selena gave him dropped onto the rug. He rolled it next to the bag with his foot. After carefully draping the coat on a chair, he flopped onto the bed, rubbed his eyes and yawned. "Mom, where are you?" He curled up in the blanket and hoped his dream would show him the truth, however ugly it might be.

He did dream, but didn't find Mom. Instead, he stood facing a massive Greek temple. Young men and girls waited at the base of the steps. Among them was Airlea, Alex's daughter in this life. He held his breath as King Aegeus's emissary called out fourteen names. Airlea was the eleventh selected. At first he thought he misheard, but Airlea stepped forward to join the other Athenian children. Alex's wife collapsed, sobbing in his arms. Their daughter would be dinner for King Minos's Minotaur.

Alex awoke with a start. "What's wrong with me? Why didn't I stop her? I never save them." In every one of Alex's past lives, there was a girl or woman in danger. He had a chance to help her, but at the pivotal moment, he faltered. "Mom, are you the one I missed saving this time?" He pressed his palms against his eyes to push the thought back. "I will find you and the Primal Key," he promised.

He trudged into Wayne's bathroom and turned on the shower to wash away the past twenty-four hours. As the room filled with steam, he swayed, his legs weakening. He managed to sit on the toilet before losing his balance. "Why can't I control them . . . ?" He stared glassy-eyed at the swirling steam, unable to find the energy to stand. A dark shape shifted behind the shower curtain. His eyes widened as a massive mist-covered bat emerged from the shower and hovered in front of him. He tossed a hand towel at it and the bat diffused into hundreds of miniature vaporous bats darting around the room. With a loud slurp, the bats collided and disappeared.

A voice coming from everywhere and nowhere filled his head.

The Primal Key must wake
Before the earths' great quake.

Alex passed out and fell off the toilet.

When he came to, Alex heard a boy's voice from inside Wayne's room. "Alex, where are you?"

Alex wondered how long he had been unconscious. He rolled onto his knees, grabbing the sink to balance.

"Alex! Come on. I'm starving," the boy said.

This time Alex recognized his cousin's voice. "Give me a minute!" Alex pulled himself up and checked his face in the mirror. No bruises, no blood; no bats; that's good, he thought. He cleaned up as best he could and joined George.

George smirked. "So, the great Alex has arrived at the estate."

"Knock it off. I'm not in the mood."

"Have you found the bottom of the Carnelian Tablet yet or are you still trying to dream up its location?" George teased.

Alex's face turned hot, not from embarrassment, but anger. He might have taken a swing at George if Anne hadn't burst into the room. She practically skipped over to him and handed him one of Dad's journals.

"I know how to save Mom. I'll jump into one of my drawings and find a time when Mom stood near it. I can tell her when Seth is going to attack our house."

"Seth has your mom?" George exclaimed. He studied his shoes. "Alex, I'm sorry. No one told me. No one ever tells me anything."

"Stop it!" Alex hissed. "Stop projecting your insecurities on us. Keep your emotions to yourself."

Alex felt George's uncertainty spike briefly to anger before turning to regret and self-doubt.

"You can't warn Mom," Alex said to Anne.

"I read how to do it in Dad's journal. I can do a lot more than you think. I —"

"Messing with the past will ruin our present and future."

Anne's face fell. "In case you haven't noticed, our present isn't going well."

"Telling her will make things worse. Seth might attack at a different time and kill Mom."

"Or Mom might find a way to keep Seth away from us — forever. You said it yourself. You don't know how to find the Key." Anne crossed her arms, waiting for Alex to suggest a better plan.

She was right. He didn't know how to save Mom or find the Key. Alex also didn't know how to tell Anne a huge steamy bat spoke to him. *Boy, that sounds ridiculous,* he realized. *I must have passed out and imagined the whole thing.* He felt George's curiosity spike. "Stay out of my thoughts —"

"I'm not eavesdropping — honest," George crouched and picked up a silver ball.

"That's mine," Alex said, snatching the ball from George.

"Actually, it's Bruegel's ball," Anne said. "Dad found two, yours and the one with ants in Isadora's office. See those creatures around your ball?" She pointed to the tiny jellyfish floating on a wavy line etched around the ball. "Dad had a special name for them." She opened a journal entitled, *Bruegelian Experiments* and flipped through the pages to find the correct section.

Alex studied Dad's sketch of Bruegel's ball. He rubbed his thumb over the raised jellyfish, wondering why Seth wanted it destroyed. "Can I keep Dad's journals for a while?"

"Okay, but I want them back before —"

Bruegel's Balls:

Possible links to:
- The Carnelian Tablet
- Alleyway Breach
- Plexian Gravity Beings
* Include in Gerald's
  next cross-dimension
  experiment

Carnelian (Amalgamators)
Fire/Rebirth
Jelly-fish found in "Triumph of Death"
under the skeleton's foot

Agate (Farmers)
Wood/Nurture
Ants found in
"Kinderspiele"
Alleyway

Amber (Alchemists)
Earth/Transform
??? Check in
"Netherlandish
Proverbs"

Onyx
(Healers)
Water/Chi
???

Crystal
(Transcenders)
Metal/Pass through
???

"Isadora's going to kill us!" George interrupted her. "We're late for her dinner party. The meal is in Anne's honor."

Alex and Anne followed George down to the main floor, through the huge reception hall and out onto the terrace. Chasca, the girl from the museum, stood by the railing. She turned and smiled at Alex. The sun had set and, behind her to the southeast, the moon was rising.

"Beautiful," Alex said, joining her. "I mean the gardens." He pointed at the courtyard in the center of the pentagon-shaped château and hoped she didn't see him blush.

"You must be Anne," Chasca said. "Isadora invited me to your New Transcender party. I'm excited to have someone my age to train with."

Anne didn't welcome this news, and remained silent as they navigated the twisting hallways to the Transcender V.I.P. dining room. Inside, ebony paneled the first eight feet of the wall, topped by a vaulted, sparkling pale green ceiling inlaid with crystals. A table set for ten occupied the center of the room where Alex's aunts and uncles sat speaking in hushed whispers.

Aunt Abigail, noticed the kids first. "Congratulations, Anne. A late bloomer, but I'm sure you will make up for lost time." She drew Anne into a suffocating hug. "I'm so very sorry about Elizabeth. It must be horrible for you. I know what a special relationship —"

Anne stepped on her foot and Abigail let out a yelp. "Sorry," Anne lied and scooted into a chair, the one farthest away from Aunt Abigail.

George's father, a burly man, chuckled. Alex liked Uncle Thomas. You knew where you stood with him. He was also

Isadora's favorite, which meant, in his quiet way, he influenced her decisions. As Alex and Chasca took the chairs beside Isadora, Uncle Wayne arrived carrying their dinner. "I made your favorite, *zuppa di pesce*."

"Fish soup is Alex's favorite, not mine," she said, quietly.

"Wayne's the finest chef in New Jersey. I'm sure the soup will taste fabulous," Aunt Abigail insisted, patting Wayne's arm a bit too hard.

Wayne tilted, nearly spilling the soup. Regaining his balance, he carefully placed the tureen on the table. "Guest of honor first." He served up Anne's bowl and proudly presented it to her.

Anne wrinkled her nose as she poked a large prawn across her bowl. She scowled. "It still has its head on."

"Swap you," George said, spearing Anne's prawn with his fork. "Do you want clams or mussels?" He pushed his bowl closer to her.

Anne covered her nose. "Pass the bread."

As Anne nibbled a roll, the adults reminisced — retelling stories . . . Thomas's first conversation with an ant — giving it directions to the kitchen . . . the time Helena used an aging elixir to get a date with an older guy in town . . . when Selena skipped lessons and took Cleopatra's Needle to Egypt. Abigail laughed. "You're lucky I found you before Isadora."

"Transcenders like their freedom," Chasca said, drawing disapproving looks from Isadora and Abigail, but

Selena smiled.

"I was grounded for a week when I left the estate without permission," Selena said "You only got three days. Isadora must be going soft in her old age."

George, who quickly consumed his dinner, began picking choice pieces from Anne's abandoned bowl.

"George — manners," Abigail snapped.

"Sorry, Mom," he muttered, slouching.

"Your emotions are leaking again," Abigail warned.

"So what if he leaks," Anne said, pushing her bowl closer to George. "They're his emotions, not yours."

"It's okay. I want to control them." George took a calming breath and pulled a smile onto his face.

Isadora shook her head in disapproval. "Given the circumstances, I will forgive your outburst — this time."

Aunt Helena opened her black clutch bag. "I'll give you a tonic to settle your nerves. "Let's see . . . time lag and spontaneous psychokinesis . . ."

"You're already animating things?" George asked Anne, trying not to stare at her.

"I didn't . . . I couldn't . . . ," Anne began to say. She didn't know what was real anymore.

"Animation is a common Amber talent. Most students have some cross-over skills," Thomas assured her and chuckled. "But, we'll be repairing hummingbirds and spiders for weeks. This almost rivals George's blizzard."

Helena triumphantly pulled a vial of purple fluid from her bag. "This should do the trick."

Alex thought Anne might bolt from the room.

"Anne's condition doesn't warrant drastic measures," Isadora said. "I'm sure her time lag will wear off by morning. She begins training with Aunt Margaret tomorrow. She'll whip her into shape."

"We'll have a great time," Chasca said.

Isadora smiled, pleased by Chasca's enthusiasm. "Your skills are progressing nicely. Your Tia Estrella would be proud."

Chasca fidgeted in her chair. "Is Tia coming to the estate?"

"No, dear," Isadora said. "She's busy in Peru studying the Nazca Lines."

Chasca leaned closer to Alex. "Over two thousand years ago, my ancestors used lines of rocks to create giant shapes. My Tia mapped the lines for the Collective. The spider is my favorite because it might mark an entrance to the Plexus."

"We're considering Estrella's theory," Isadora said. "I plan to test it myself once we find the Key. For now, I asked your aunt to take a break from the spider. A recent sandstorm exposed new biomorphs and geoglyphs. A 100-foot-long bat interests me most."

Alex, devouring a second bowl of Uncle Wayne's *zuppa di pesce*, swallowed a clam whole. Holding his throat, he croaked out, "Bat?" He reached for his glass and guzzled the water.

Isadora's eyes narrowed to study Alex. "Yes, the biomorph resembles the symbols on the top edge of the tablets."

"Do bats bother you Alex?" Thomas asked.

Alex pushed his last prawn around his plate. He knew he couldn't keep secrets from Thomas for long. His uncle was an Agate Tablet master. "A bat invaded my shower. It said I had to wake up the Primal Key before a giant earthquake." There, he said it. He didn't care if they thought he was crazy — which they clearly did.

Isadora spoke first. "More than a century ago, a creature, a massive bat, visited Lady Brunel. It told her to connect the tablets and find the Primal Key. It also foretold the birth of a bold Amalgamator — someone who would trigger death and destruction."

CHAPTER NINE

AUNT MARGARET'S TRAVEL TIPS

Anne plopped down on her mom's old bed. She couldn't relax. The bed looked beautiful, but the mattress was hard and smelled like cleaning chemicals. Dinner was miserable. Even worse, she was sure Alex was developing a crush on Chasca. Chasca acted nice enough, but Anne knew her type. Alex would fall for her glamour and phony kindness, then she would discard him the moment he no longer suited her. He was supposed to be able to see into the future. Why couldn't he see Chasca meant heartbreak? If Mom were here, she'd knock some sense into him. Mom — Anne ached to see her. She glanced at the steps leading to Mom's laboratory. I can't — not yet. It was hard enough staying in Mom's room. The room was sterile, lacking Mom's compassion, spontaneity and strength.

She rolled over and picked up one of Dad's journals: *Pieter Bruegel the Elder's Child's Play: The Dangers Lurking in the Alleyway*. In the first section, Dad had sketched Bruegel's kids playing games. Anne recognized leapfrog, rolling hoops and playing with dolls, but the game called "blowing up a pig's bladder" sounded disgusting—even if the result was a medieval version of a balloon. When she reached a game Dad called, "The Devil's Tail," she understood the journal's title. Boys and girls lined up, each holding another's shirttail, as they emerged from an alleyway onto the main street. Dad circled the third girl's face and jotted a note. "Bridget, the first Transcender to lose her way in Bruegel's pigment breach."

Anne slapped the book shut and slid the Bruegel journal onto the nightstand. She picked up *Mastering the Crystal Tablet* to re-read the section on scanning and sifting time in paintings. She didn't care what Alex believed. Tomorrow she would learn how to warn Mom. Mom would fix everything. Her eyes tired and, after a few pages, she curled up with Fosby Bear and fell asleep.

She dreamed about Seth's agents breaking into her Collinsville home. It was as if she had been there instead of running around Central Park with Bixia. A deafening explosion rocked the house, knocking Anne to the ground. She curled into a ball, her arms raised to protect her head. When the ringing in her ears subsided, she slowly opened her eyes. Her home was gone. The air tasted of decay and death. In a dingy tunnel, Mom huddled on the floor, a half-eaten sandwich and an empty water bottle beside her. Anne choked back a sob at the depth of despair in her mother's face.

She called out, "Mom, where are we?"

Her mother jerked her head in Anne's direction, as her piercing green eyes frantically searched for her daughter.

"Mom, I can't hear you," Anne shrieked, watching her mother try to speak.

A tremor shook the tunnel. The roof collapsed, sealing Mom behind a mound of stone. A breeze blew through the hole in the ceiling. Anne knew she needed help. She scrambled up the rocks. A Federal stone building, much like the White House, lay in ruins in front of her. The air was fresh, but a misty night fog chilled her. In the distance, the sky glowed in patches — a town, she guessed. She took a few tentative steps into the overgrown lawn. The world shook again, harder this time. The grass turned into sand covered with red-brown rock. With a roar, louder than a hundred jet engines, the ground split, tumbling Anne into a fiery abyss. As flames singed her hair, the winged beast from Isadora's meditation room, swooped above her. It snagged her in its claws. Sizzling with lightning, it flew over the inferno. It dove, slicing through a canopy of luminous spider webs blanketing a putrid, greenish-gray river oozing through the fire.

"The Curse is upon us. Stop the Amalgamator. Awaken the Key," the translucent spiders lamented, trying to repair their webs.

The beast circled preparing for another attack, but a geyser erupted from the river, knocking the creature off balance.

It screeched, spun out of control and dropped Anne to die in flames.

Anne awoke, her skin still burning from the fire.

"Come on, Anne," Alex said, pushing Anne's shoulder. "You already missed breakfast. Soon you'll be late for training. You'd better hurry. Isadora called. She wants you in her office, and she sounds pretty cranky."

Anne pulled the covers over her head and wrapped the pillow around her ears. She wished the winged monster and Isadora's training agenda were both dreams, but they weren't. She crawled out of bed, grabbed clean clothes and retreated into Mom's bathroom.

"I finished reading Dad's Bruegel experiments journal. Did you know Gerald was an Amalgamator?" Alex asked through the door.

"Uh-uh," Anne sputtered through toothpaste. Anne thought of the spider's warning and the Bat's message. Could Alex be the Amalgamator who would cause death and destruction?

"George told me no one has tried the experiments since Gerald disappeared."

"You mean murdered — like Grandpa," Anne muttered, wiping the stray toothpaste from her lips.

"Gerald thought Bruegel possessed alchemy, transcending and amalgamating talents."

"How? He didn't have the tablets," Anne said, emerging from the bathroom.

"Don't know, but I'm going to try to channel Bruegel's spirit."

"Alex, he's dangerous!"

"He's dead. If he's still a ghost, the worst he can do is possess me."

Anne opened *Child's Play: Dangers Lurking in the Alleyway* to show Alex the picture of Bridget. "Bruegel's painting swallows up Transcenders."

"Then I won't visit his paintings. I've been thinking. What if the Bat's great earthquake is the one Seth plans to cause? The Bat wants me to find the Primal Key in time to save Mom — Bruegel is my best lead."

"Do you hear yourself? How do you know the Bat's right — or honest?"

"I'll hate myself if I don't try everything possible to find it. Come on, Isadora is waiting." Alex led the way down the stairs to the shadowy hallway with the single door to Isadora's suite.

"You said Isadora was in her office —" Anne's legs tingled. She scowled at Alex, grabbed his hand and pulled him through the wall. "Why didn't you tell me about the portal?" she complained as they stepped into Isadora's office.

"Isadora told me not to," Alex objected.

Isadora greeted them sternly. "You're late. Alex, go to the artifact room while I have a word with Anne." Alex hesitated, staring at one of the palm-sized, bronze leopards on the bookshelf. "He only bit you once." Isadora huffed. "Stand up to him or he won't let you through." Isadora grabbed the leopard. It growled and lashed its tail as she slid it across the shelf. With a click, the bookcase opened. Alex disappeared down the circular steps into the bowels of the building.

"I understand you missed breakfast. I have tea and biscuits if you're hungry," Isadora offered.

83

Anne accepted the tea and sat in the cushy, wingback chair. Everywhere she looked, she saw precious trinkets. How did Isadora cram all this stuff into one room and still keep it looking tidy with everything in its correct place? Not quite everything, though, she decided. Anne's eyes lingered on an easel where a black cloth shrouded a painting.

Isadora stepped in front of the easel blocking her view. "I'm showing some students the gemstone tablets. You may join us. Then I want you with Aunt Margaret for lessons." From her desk, Isadora picked up the crazy-key charm bracelet and draped it across her hand. "You have catch-up work to do. Your uncontrolled powers are dangerous."

"That bracelet is what's dangerous," Anne said, forcing a laugh to hide her fear. The closer Isadora came with it, the more Anne wanted to run. She placed her mug on the side table and sat on her hands. No way, she thought. I refuse.

Isadora continued to stare at the bracelet. "I have no idea what you think it did . . . . Well, it doesn't matter for now. Margaret convinced me you should master the basics first."

Isadora tossed the bracelet onto her desk. She led Anne through the opened bookcase and down the stairs. They descended four stories before reaching a polished metal door. "This is our artifact room. It is the safest, most secure room on the estate. If anything goes wrong, make your way here."

"Can it protect me from a massive earthquake that opens a chasm to the earth's core," Anne asked, thinking of her dream.

"That might test it a bit," Isadora said with a smile.

"I thought so," Anne muttered.

Inside the room a sculpture hung above a circular table. Alex, Chasca, George and two other students sat studying old parchments.

Isadora pressed a button, and the sculpture lowered. "These are the actual gemstone tablets." She motioned to the students. "Come take a closer look."

"What do the symbols mean?" Anne asked, scanning the rows and columns of glyphs.

Isadora chuckled. "I wish we knew. We've translated sixty-three percent of them — enough to master some talents. We won't understand the tablet's full powers until we find a way to connect them." She pushed the edge of the opaque Amber Tablet, rotating it to show its bottom. "Olivia, what does the largest symbol mean?" she asked a thin girl with a long neck and intense blue eyes.

Olivia leaned over to examine the symbol through its Plexiglas case. "Thoth represents the essence of what we learn from the Amber Tablet. He helps us understand the nature of all things and evolve them into their divine state."

"Well said," Isadora praised.

Anne's face softened as an early memory surfaced. "Thoth is the church key!"

"Church key?" Isadora asked.

"Yes, a beer bottle opener. That's what Grandpa called it whenever he read me his book. "You see," Anne recited happily:

"Thoth uses his church key to open a passage to Egypt.

In China, the chi flag flies to bring you good health.

85

The antique antenna can provide you the greatest reception in Crete. In Mexico, a hamburger-man whisks you through customs.

And, you must always use the funky looking toothbrushes when you're visiting the Indus Valley."

Olivia giggled, but Chasca looked disgusted as if Anne was making fun of something sacred.

A bittersweet smile crossed Isadora's face. "How can you possibly remember? You were five."

Olivia held her hand above the church key. "Thoth does more than transport you to Egypt. This tablet tells you how to make lead into gold."

The other student, a boy named Bakari, said, "I thought the Emerald Tablet —"

"The Emerald Tablet was the first draft for this one," Olivia explained. Unable to contain her excitement, she asked, "Do you have a philosopher's stone?"

Isadora scoffed. "Of course not — dreadful things those stones — and you know the tablets teach us a great deal more than how to extend human lifespans —"

"Like the Assassins' spells on the Onyx Tablet," Bakari interjected, wanting to show he knew as much as Olivia.

Isadora nodded her approval and moved around the sculpture. "This is the Crystal Tablet Darwin uncovered along the Acula River in Mexico." Chasca nudged Anne aside to stand closer to Isadora.

Isadora traced her hand over the Epi-Olmec script. "What Hubert called a Mexican hamburger-man is the symbol for 'they pass.' This tablet taught us to travel in time and, one day, if we learn enough, to enter the Plexus. Chasca and Anne, this is your tablet. Your skills are rare. Only nineteen active Transcenders remain in the Collective."

Anne thought of the missing girl, Bridget, and wondered how many Transcenders lost their way or died horribly.

"I don't see bat symbols?" Alex said, leaning over the tablet.

Isadora spun the tablet for Alex to see the bats flitting across the top edge of the gemstones. She spun it again. "The other edges have glyphs unique to each tablet."

Anne looked at a glyph on the Crystal Tablet's side. On top of a snake's body, a fish head opened its mouth, exposing fang-like teeth. "What is that thing?"

"Abigail nicknamed it the viperfish. We're still looking for its shape in the Nazca Lines." Isadora moved to the next tablet to continue the introductory lesson. "The Agate Tablet is from the Indus Valley. It teaches us cross-species communication, climate management techniques, and for most students," she said, glancing at George, "containing and influencing emotions."

Olivia smiled. "You mean George can make me believe anything he wants?"

Isadora raised an eyebrow and scoffed. "Maybe one day, but such applications would be an irresponsible use of power."

George studied his shoes and muttered, "Simon's the best at it. You should be careful around him."

Anne smiled at the tiny ant glyphs crawling on the tablet, remembering how Simon kept the insects away from her. She gently bit her lower lip. She felt safe with Simon, but now wondered if the emotion was real.

Isadora paused ceremoniously over a red tablet. "Lady Anne Brunel procured the Carnelian Tablet for the family in 1842. The Linear B symbols explain life beyond death and rebirth."

"Do you mean true immortality?" Olivia asked.

"Yes, but critical parts are missing so we can't form testable theories. Somewhere in the past, this tablet was whole. If we can find the missing symbols, I'm certain we can connect the message across the five tablets and find the Primal Key." Isadora crossed the room to a cabinet.

Alex leaned over the Carnelian Tablet to examine the edge. He waved for Anne to join him and pointed at the jelly-fish-shaped symbols.

"Bruegel's ball," she whispered. "If the jellyfish are Plexians, the other glyphs must be, too."

Isadora returned with two palm-sized leather cases. "These are CyberNexuses." Anne and Alex reached for the devices, but Isadora pulled her hand back. "Don't lose or damage them. While you're at the estate, I want you to record your progress. The devices combine personal comm-pad features and field research tools." She flipped one open to display the five tiers of controls.

George, who already owned a CyberNexus, activated his electronic assistant — a black stallion hologram trotting across the display.

"They are not toys," Isadora snapped. George quickly closed the device.

"Time for your lessons," Isadora said and led the way out of the artifact room, leaving Alex to study Linear B symbols. Anne followed reluctantly. Please be careful with Bruegel, she silently begged Alex.

As Isadora whisked them through a series of corridors, Bakari asked, "May I go to The Met today?"

"Yes, Emma told me The Met is secured. She will meet you at the Temple of Dendur. I want you to study the Magical Stela."

"The Stela? But I was working on poisons —"

"You spend too much time on the Assassins' spells. It's high time you focused on healing." Isadora ignored Bakari's sulking and addressed Olivia. "I want a fresh batch of Egyptian Blue and Smalt ready by this evening. Wayne collected the Heliopolis sand and phoenix ashes this morning."

"Those pigments are complex. It will take me hours," Olivia said happily. "Thank you for trusting me. I'll brew, I mean do, my best."

Waves of misery flowed off George as Isadora turned her attention to him. "Control your emotions or go home," Isadora scolded him. "In this state you will fail your first test — again."

His shame mixed with fear. Isadora's nagging made him even more nervous. "Don't worry," Anne said, gently touching his arm as they entered the meditation room. "You'll pass your Level One test today. I'm sure." She put as much confidence as she could manage behind her words. A smile crossed George's face.

Isadora stopped, facing Aunt Margaret's portrait. "Anne, please find a nice place to land and picture yourself in the composition. If you have problems, Chasca can help you."

As soon as Isadora and the other students left, Chasca popped into the painting. Anne glanced around the meditation room to pick a place to return. In front of Grandpa, she decided, taking in the details. Satisfied she would remember, she faced Aunt Margaret. Delicate clematis vines framed her painting. She wore jeans and a red sweater that complimented her white hair. Rugged and determined, a walking stick in one hand, she appeared ready to climb the pathway winding up the grassy, autumn hillside. Despite Alex's dire warning against changing the past to influence the future, Anne would contact Mom today. She took a deep breath and imagined standing under the largest maple tree near Margaret. Unlike her clean entry into the crayon drawing, thick, murky layers of oil paint pulled at her skin. The paint still tingled her face when she landed. Anne saw Chasca, hands on her hips, standing beside Margaret.

"Welcome to my world," Margaret said.

Shocked, Anne stumbled backward. Margaret spoke and moved. Birds chirped and soft breezes rustled the tree leaves. Even the grass crunched under Anne's feet. "May I talk? Isadora said people in the past would hear me," Anne whispered, hoping she didn't ruin someone's future.

Chasca smirked. "The gag rule applies to normal paintings."

Margaret laughed. "A little haunting does have its advantages, though. Here, your words and thoughts imprint in my paint."

"All my thoughts?" Anne asked nervously.

"No, you exchange the thoughts you want others to hear, but be careful, holding your tongue is easier than keeping your mind from wandering. Let's take a walk. There is a nice clearing beneath those trees that overlooks the valley."

At the top of the hill, birch trees surrounded an outcrop of rocks marking the edge of a steep cliff. The cliff overlooked a bowl-shaped valley surrounded by soft, rounded mountains.

Yellow, orange and red trees reflected on the glassy, smooth lake at the valley's center. A waterfall glistened as it cut a way through a distant mountain in three cascades before plunging into the river feeding the lake.

"Where are we?" Anne asked.

"The Catskills. As a child, I spent summers in a cabin near the lake. By the time Isadora created my painting, developers had ruined the valley. So I chose to have my portrait set over the hill. Isadora painted the landscape where I stand for those in the physical world to see, but I created this valley based on my memories."

"You made the entire valley?" Anne asked.

"We applied some tablet principles to develop special pigments. The results have been life changing. Enough about my painting, you're here to time-travel. Let's get down to business. Entering a painting is the hardest part, but you managed that nicely. Once you are inside, the two easiest ways to navigate portals are —"

"Scan and sift and the direct jump," Chasca quickly answered.

Margaret nodded. "Not exciting names, but descriptive enough. Now, brace yourself," Margaret said and held Anne's hand. "Chasca, try to keep up with us."

Margaret's painting swirled and blurred, the colors combining, until everything was black. Although Margaret still gripped Anne's hand, she could see nothing. The nothingness seeped into Anne's mind muddling her thoughts. A speck of light appeared. It expanded into a wobbly line.

"We're nearing the edge of the Void," Margaret said. "When the light twists and splits, focus on the first image you see."

Anne's body vibrated. Too many sounds for her mind to

discern blared in her ears. When the light split, a kaleidoscope of faces and strange rooms crashed above her in waves.

"Stop struggling," Margaret yelled. She lost her grip.

Anne's body tumbled toward the torrent of images. Terrified, she pictured the meditation room and landed in a heap by Grandpa's portrait. Anne took a moment to catch her breath before facing Margaret's painting. She didn't want to go back inside, but she needed to learn to sift time. She landed under the maple tree and found Margaret, pacing. Chasca sat on a boulder near the cliff.

"What should I tell Isadora?" Chasca asked.

"She could be anywhere in the past . . . or lost in the Void. Lord help her if she reached the Plexus. She wouldn't survive a minute," Margaret said. She looked up and saw Anne. "You're alive!" Margaret hugged her tightly. "How did you —"

"It was horrible — the sounds . . . faces . . . and smells. How do I make them stop?" Anne asked.

"You mean you didn't find a focal point?" Chasca grinned. "I'm surprised you're not puking."

"This is a serious matter," Margaret scolded.

Chasca tried to look ashamed — Anne knew she was faking it. Now that Anne was safe, Chasca found her mistake amusing.

"It was as bad as wearing Isadora's bracelet," Anne thought. "At least I didn't see any monsters."

As Margaret had warned, Anne's stray thoughts turned to words.

"Isadora told me you borrowed the bracelet," Margaret said, sternly.

Anne nervously rubbed her wrist.

Chasca came to Anne's rescue, although Anne guessed it was for her own self-serving reasons.

"May I test for my level-three?" she asked.

"How far back did you research?" Margaret asked, taking her attention off Anne for the moment.

"Thirty-five years," Chasca said, eagerly.

"Twenty years ago, my painting was placed in storage for minor repair. Figure out who — other than Isadora — knew the location of the storage room."

Thrilled, Chasca disappeared.

"Chasing Isadora through time should keep her busy for the rest of the day. Come," Margaret said, reaching for Anne's hand. Anne pulled away. "Not a trip to the Void this time," Margaret promised. "We will take a tiny hop inside my world."

Margaret led Anne to the cliff. "Ever dream of flying?" she asked and stepped off the edge. Air rushed up, blowing Anne's hair into the air. Margaret grinned as Anne spread her arms wide, enjoying the rush of freefall. When Anne could see the individual leaves on the treetops, the air crackled then split. Margaret slowed their descent, gently floating into the valley. They touched down on a narrow beach along the lake.

Margaret pointed to a weathered picnic table near a crop of trees. "I designed the crazy-key bracelet sitting at that table. Your mother sparked the idea in my mind. When Elizabeth was young, she loved coming to my painting for lessons, even though transcending didn't come naturally to her. Every Saturday we would swim in my lake. She was floating on her back and gazing at the cloudless sky when she said, 'We must link the tablets — but we can't.'

"'Yes, Elizabeth,' I replied. 'I know the Carnelian Tablet must be repaired before we can find the Primal Key.' She flipped over and stared at me. 'Try channeling all five — together.' Then she splashed me in the face and dove underwater."

Anne's mother hated the estate. It was strange to think she spent Saturdays happily swimming with Margaret.

Margaret continued. "That night the extended family met. Cross-tablet talents are rare. It took Isadora thirty-four years of dedicated training to master three. But your mother and Selena showed multiple skills before they could walk. If we could magnify their talents, we thought they might see the higher dimensions and find a way to reach the Plexus. Elizabeth was thrilled."

"Then why did Mom quit the Collective?"

"It was the pigments. She hated brewing paints for Isadora, but she made the best ones — such a waste of talent. I spent three months designing the bracelet for Elizabeth and Selena. As you know, it did nothing. Your grandfather claimed his daughters weren't crazy enough to make them work. Anne, are you crazy enough to try?"

"No! The monster is real — I know it is."

"Pity. It might help save Elizabeth. If you speed up your development, you might discover clues to your mother's location. Besides, if I'm correct, your monster can only breach points where his dimension touches ours. Hubert designed his portrait to tether higher dimensions. Stay clear of it and we shouldn't have any unwanted guests."

Anne knew when someone was manipulating her, but this time the prize was too big to ignore. If the bracelet could help her warn Mom, she would take the risk. "In one of Dad's journals he mentions quick jumps to the past. Is it difficult? Could the bracelet help me?"

"You don't need help. You already possess the skills. To jump into the past you must know the destination from a prior scanning or by researching the ownership history of the painting. Either way, you focus on a detail, a face or a room where the painting hung, and jump. But you must follow the gag rule or you will influence the past."

"Change can be good," Anne suggested.

"Not often," Margaret warned and rubbed a long-healed wound on her side.

An idea came to Anne — one that didn't risk ruining the past or creating a worse future. "Can I jump to places I have never visited — places from my dreams?"

"Your father believed it was possible."

"Last night I dreamt an explosion trapped Mom underground."

"Do you know where?"

"No, but it was near the ruins of a stone building."

"I understand your artistic skills are excellent. Perhaps you should journal your dreams and sketch what you remember." Margaret studied Anne for a moment before asking, "Are you ready to try?"

Anne nodded, knowing this choice would change her — forever.

"Before your afternoon lesson, I want you to study his journals. Your father and Gerald discovered a way to transport objects between the physical and imagined worlds. He sent me such thoughtful presents. One day a real apple bobbed across my lake.

It was a deliciously tart Granny Smith. I created an orchard based on that memory. But such skills require years of training. Unless . . ." Margaret glanced at Anne's wrist. "Retrieve the bracelet and ask Isadora for a swimsuit. From now on, we work in the lake. Water is the safest place to experiment," Margaret said with a mischievous smile.

CHAPTER TEN

BRUEGEL'S PIGMENTS

Aunt Margaret and Anne stood waist-deep in the water watching the rock-strewn muck of the lakebed churn as a whirlpool collapsed. Anne smacked her hand against the water. For hours, Anne had tried — and failed — to use the bracelet to open a window between Margaret's painting and the physical world. This time, for a moment, Mom's room in the mansion swirled at the base of the vortex, but it quickly distorted and disappeared.

"Let's try starting at the lakebed and funnel the water toward the sky," Margaret suggested.

"I'm too cold and tired." Anne complained.

"You look a bit pale. Perhaps, after a longer rest, you will have the energy to break through."

Anne drip-dried on the beach, while Aunt Margaret stoked a bonfire with driftwood until it blazed blue. A stiff breeze peppered Anne with sand. She shivered, goose bumps forming on her arms, and huddled by the fire pit.

Margaret spread a pink towel on the ground and sat beside Anne. "After dinner, review your father's journals. We must be doing something wrong."

"I've read *The Art of Transcending* six times. I'm sure I conjured the whirlpool correctly. Maybe I'm too weak — even with the bracelet."

"Nonsense. Try sending me a treat from Elizabeth's room. It might be easier from the physical side." Margaret tossed a log on the bonfire, shooting up sparks. In the embers by the log, a woman's face emerged and asked, "Where am I?"

"Isadora, you're awake!" Margaret applauded.

Isadora tried to push the flames aside. "This is not what I expected."

"It seldom is. No matter how many times you hear the stories, you can't prepare. Each awakening is unique. Excuse me for moment while I finish Anne's lesson." Margaret led Anne a few steps away from Isadora. "Before you return to the meditation room, I have an errand for you." Margaret nodded toward the fire and whispered, "Check on Isadora's self-portrait. Let me know how she is fairing. How she adapts during the first few days affects the stability of her world."

"Isadora's portrait is alive?"

"Awake," Margaret corrected. "Isadora's at a vulnerable stage

98

in her development, but you should be able to reach her world through the bonfire." Seeing Anne's alarm, she quickly added, "You will be fine. The bracelet will improve your chances. When you find Isadora's world, hop across the time-stream."

Anne took a tentative step toward the fire pit. The wood crackled and popped, warming her skin. She glanced back at Margaret who gave her an encouraging nod. Anne, holding her breath, and shielding her face with her hand, stepped into the embers. The charred wood crunched under her feet as the flames shifted to let her pass — unburned.

Within Margaret's world, the fire pit spanned no more than six feet, but inside the curtain of flames, a kaleidoscope of paintings twisted. The family portraits from Isadora's meditation room and many other unfamiliar faces lit up and flickered out like fireflies. Grandpa's face illuminated. He smiled and shook his head in amusement. "You're full of surprises," he said.

Isadora's self-portrait swirled near him. He blew her a kiss, but she turned away.

A narrow, murky brook cut through the fire separating Anne from Isadora's world. Stepping across the time-stream looked easy, but she couldn't take her eyes off the shifting, shadowy water. Growing dizzy and disoriented, Anne sank into the embers. I'll rest for a moment, she decided. Mesmerized, she watched as the brook flooded into a stream spewing steam and hissing through the bonfire. The stream wound around Anne isolating her on an island of glowing cinders.

Isadora's self-portrait yelled. "The Expanse is opening. Don't look down. You must jump!"

The stream churned violently and widened. Anne staggered

to her feet, stepped back a few paces, ran and leaped as far as she could manage. She landed in a shadowy room with a single chair and a dying fire in the hearth. The painted version of Isadora sat on the floor in the corner.

"You waited too long," Isadora scolded, swirling her finger in circles across the floor. "Your bulk caused ripples then made waves."

Anne laughed, looking at her skinny body. She wished she weighed more — in the right places, of course.

Isadora looked in Anne's direction, but focused on the wall instead of her face. "Cross-painting jumps turn perilous if you hesitate. Those streams are infinitely deep. If you miss the other side, you fall — forever." Isadora brushed her hands on her pants, carefully stood and shuffled to the chair. She groaned as she sat.

Anne glanced away. This Isadora didn't measure up to the real thing.

"I look ragged — I know," Isadora said. "Did Margaret send you to make sure I'm sane? Well, I am . . . . She shouldn't have . . . . You're not ready to jump between paintings . . . . I guess that's my fault . . . . I should have recognized your potential sooner."

Wanting to avoid Isadora's erratic gaze, Anne glanced around the stark room. It reminded her of the gloomy hallway leading to Isadora's suite. "Why didn't you paint yourself somewhere fun?"

"Isadora couldn't risk adding me into Hubert's portrait with inferior pigments. I'm not ready for visitors, you see." Isadora's longing gaze rested on a red door.

Anne watched the door ripple, as if it wasn't sure which world it belonged to. "What's in there?"

"Anything I can imagine, but I haven't decided what to construct. I might not have the power to manifest objects in my world."

"Margaret created such a wonderful —"

Isadora huffed. "Margaret stood, stuck on her painted hillside for decades, until Elizabeth improved Lady Brunel's pigments and washes. I saved every drop Elizabeth made for Hubert. He required more than I expected. When I completed his portrait, only a single vial of Carmine Lake pigment remained. Isadora used it for my fire and door."

Anne cringed. "How could you let Isadora do this to you — to herself?"

"I — I mean — she will leave for Nazca soon. Estrella reported unusual readings near the spider. They match the energy Seth used to contain your portal. We can't take risks — she knows too much. If she dies at Nazca, I'm the only recording of her life — even if I'm imperfect." Isadora hurried to add, "It's not her fault, though. She didn't know the pigments would affect my mind. She'll fix me when we get Elizabeth back home . . . . But we can't trade the Key for Elizabeth. Seth would unleash horrors into our world." Isadora shook her head, sadly. "I wish the Key never existed."

As Anne pulled the bracelet off and turned to leave, Isadora whimpered in pain. She looked at Anne and pleaded, "You'll help convince Elizabeth — won't you? Ask her to stay at the estate . . . . She can make more pigments . . . . She can't leave me like this." Isadora abruptly stood and returned to her corner. "You should go. Another upwelling is coming." The red door warped and twisted. "Leave, now!"

Anne grimaced and jumped into the meditation room. She accidently bumped into Simon, tumbling them to the floor. "Sorry!" Anne blushed as she quickly rolled off him.

Simon laughed and offered Anne a hand up. "You should look both ways before jumping. Traffic is relatively slow here, but if you exit a museum piece without checking, you'll hurt someone. I guess Bixia didn't teach you Portal Protocol #2: Proper Precautions Prevent Pain."

Anne smiled, comforted by his presence, then remembered she was wearing the horrible red-ruffled bathing suit Isadora supplied her. She looked, frantically, for the cover-up she stashed.

"Your robe's over there," Simon said, pointing where her robe lay, neatly folded, on the table beneath Isadora's self-portrait."

Anne looked into Isadora's confident eyes and wondered if the woman inside would recover. She pulled on the robe, cinching the belt tight.

"Marcus asked me to find you," Simon said. "He wants to talk with you before you see your mom again."

Anne's eyes darted to the wall where her crayon drawing hung. Had Alex told Marcus her plan to warn Mom? Was Simon here to stop her? The comfort of being in Simon's presence strengthened. He's probing my thoughts she realized and pushed her plan from her mind, focusing instead on her horrible bathing suit.

Simon grinned and placed his hand between her shoulders, gently pushing her toward the Thoth door. He escorted her to Isadora's office where Marcus sat at the desk, a data pad in his hands. Bixia leaned against a bookcase, scratching one of the leopards under its chin. Content, the cat caressed Bixia's wrist with its tail.

"I see you've been swimming with Margaret," Bixia said. "Have any revelations down by the lake?"

"Not yet," Anne said, pulling the bracelet out of her bathing suit.

"Give it time. Margaret will help you own your powers," Bixia replied, crossing to a large canvas shrouded under black cloth.

As Bixia pulled the cloth off the canvas, Anne gasped and backed away from the painting. "The kids, they're running around like crazy, and the adults don't even care."

"You see them moving?" Bixia asked.

The children's faces melted, morphing into translucent spiders and ants, scurrying toward the bottom of the landscape.

"They're going to escape. Do something!" Anne exclaimed, pointing at the painting.

"The kids are stuck inside. There's no doorway out for them," Bixia assured her.

Simon reached for Anne's hand. "Drop the bracelet."

Anne shoved it into the pocket of her robe. The chaos of the painting subsided, eventually freezing into place. Anne took a step closer. She recognized the boy and girl rolling hoops with sticks. "*Kinderspiele*," she whispered.

Bixia folded the black cloth and placed it on Isadora's desk. "Your dad was obsessed with Bruegel's living paintings, a good thing, too, or Isadora wouldn't have arranged to borrow this one — the detail is extraordinary, even better than Aunt Margaret's world. I wish we had the recipes for his pigments."

"Why would Dad want a deadly painting?"

"Do you see the bonfire way down the road?" Bixia asked pointing to the center of the canvas. "Bruegel created a transportation hub to his other paintings there."

"Like the fire in Margaret's painting," Anne said.

"After your Dad discovered Bruegel's fires, your Mom designed a Carmine Lake pigment almost as good as Bruegel's." Bixia squared her body in front of the painting.

"You're going inside *Kinderspiele*? But the alleyway —"

Bixia disappeared.

"Why didn't you stop her?" Anne asked Marcus.

"Bixia's our best agent. She accepts the risks. Thanks to Seth's fascination with Bruegel, Bixia used the painting hub to locate seventeen of his bases. I hope one of them resembles the buildings in your dream."

"My dream? How . . ."

"Margaret can't keep a secret. I'm sure the entire Collective knows by now." Marcus handed his data pad to Anne. The first image, an industrial complex along a river, looked nothing like the ruins in her dream. She shook her head and swiped her finger across the screen. In the next image, a villa perched on a cliff above the ocean.

"No —" A soothing warmth grew in her chest, disrupting her thoughts. Recognizing its source, she quickly turned to catch Simon staring at her.

Marcus jerked his head and glared at Simon. "You're a

distraction. Go practice climate manipulation. I want to see your rainstorm this evening — without lightening this time."

As Simon left, Anne sensed his annoyance, which he quickly repressed. She returned her attention to the remaining images. Nothing looked promising. "Will Bixia find more bases?"

"For now, she's visiting the ones we know. This morning Seth arrived at his ranch in Texas." Marcus pulled up the aerial view of the Spanish Mission style mansion. "You're sure this isn't the one?"

Anne shook her head. Although the exterior of the building was white like the one in her dream, she was certain Seth imprisoned Mom beneath the ruins of a Federal Style building twenty-times the size of Seth's mansion. "If I go with Bixia, I might find the right base —"

"No! *Kinderspiele* is too dangerous. It can become an endless maze. We lost Bridget — I won't risk you."

Frustrated, Anne shoved her hands into her pockets, accidently pressing against the bracelet. Her legs began to tingle and a ringing came from the portals in Isadora's office as they opened. Anne could see straight through each one. She pulled away from the bracelet, and the portals melted back into bookcases. As she squinted at the remaining rippling vapor where they existed, heat prickled up her spine and settled at the base of her skull. Anne let Marcus probe her thoughts, but it annoyed her he didn't ask first.

"You sense me inside your mind?" Marcus asked. "You're right, I should ask permission."

As Marcus withdrew, Anne's neck cooled.

"I knew you were aware of Simon's interest, but chalked it

105

up to intuition. Recognizing a probe is a true Agate talent. I will ask Thomas to begin your cross-tablet training tomorrow."

"I don't want Agate talents or more training! I want Mom back!" Before Marcus could reply, Anne turned and sprinted through the portal leading to Isadora's suite in the mansion.

Although exhausted from a full day of training, she stomped up the steps to Mom's room, muttering. "I don't want more talents . . . . I can't even control the ones I have . . . . Nothing I'm doing will help Mom, Marcus doesn't have a clue where she is and Alex will never find the Key in time . . . . Even if he does . . ." Anne stopped and stared at Mom's bedroom door. "Isadora will never give in to Seth's demands. The painted Isadora said so herself. Isadora doesn't care about Mom!" Anne pushed the door open and strode into the room. Isadora wouldn't save Mom, but the mentally unstable woman in her self-portrait needed Mom's pigments. An overwhelming desire to know what Mom created in the lab swelled inside Anne. She rushed up the steps — taking them two at a time.

In Mom's lab, a telescope on a raised platform dominated the room, but it didn't interest Anne. She circled the platform past walls of storage cabinets, until she reached Mom's workstation. Dust covered the table and chemistry apparatus. Against the wall, shelves held hundreds of books and a single, framed, black and white etching. Although Anne meant to search Mom's lab for anything that might help the ailing, painted Isadora, she couldn't pull her eyes away from the etching. An alchemist worked at his desk as smoke plumed from his stove. Outside, a woman with three children tried to escape the complex. Although Anne couldn't read most of the words along the bottom of the scene, she recognized Bruegel's signature and her dad's writing beneath it, "For my Alchemist. All my love, Matthew."

A smile spread across Anne's face as she realized Mom saw this etching sometime in the past. Anne studied the area around the workstation, picking the exact place to return. "I hope Bruegel didn't invent living inks." She crossed her fingers, focused on the youngest child in the etching, and jumped.

Thankfully, like her crayon drawing, the scene remained static. As Margaret taught her, Anne opened the Void and focused on one detail, Mom's smile — nothing. Try a key word, she decided, and listened for the name "Elizabeth." Thousands of windows into time rolled in waves above her. I can't fall out of the etching, she told herself trying to keep her head from swimming in dizzying circles. She focused, instead, on the word, "Bruegel," and the windows faded until nine openings remained.

"Bruegel's experiments? Mother, how could you!" Anne heard Mom yell from the closest window. Anne peered inside. A much younger Mom, probably in her twenties, stood beside a man with clear blue eyes and honey blonde hair. Isadora sat at Mom's workstation — arms crossed and wearing a stern expression.

"Where are my pigments," Elizabeth demanded. "They're not ready — they could be deadly."

"You're lying to me," Isadora said calmly. "I tested them last night. What else are you hiding from me?"

"Nothing," Elizabeth muttered. "You got what you wanted, now leave."

Elizabeth waited, silently, until Isadora descended the stairs and closed the bedroom door behind her. "She's gone too far this time. I'm leaving the estate and taking Bruegel's recipes with me." She pulled a journal from the shelf. Anne recognized it immediately — *Responsible Art: Avoiding Deadly Results* — one of the journals from the box in her attic; the journal Selena never found.

"Will you leave tonight?" the blond man asked.

Mom nodded, her jaw clenched tight.

"I'll coming with you," he said, drawing Elizabeth into his arms. She leaned her head on his chest.

"Matthew, you can't — your work."

"Means nothing if I'm not with you."

"Dad?" Anne whispered.

"Isadora won't let us go without a fight," Elizabeth said.

"We'll be gone before she knows it. If we reach Thomas's hideout on Bear Island before SANDY notices, Selena can portal us off the estate." Matthew kissed Elizabeth's forehead. "How does Paris sound?"

"Wonderful," Elizabeth replied, the tension releasing from her shoulders.

Matthew, his arm still around her waist, led Elizabeth toward the stairs.

"Wait!" Anne yelled.

They turned, searching for an intruder.

"I'm inside the Bruegel etching," Anne called out.

"Isadora sent a spy," Elizabeth growled, striding across the room. She yanked the etching off the bookcase. "You're about to discover how it feels to be damaged in a work of art."

"Mom! I have to warn you about Seth —" Anne cried as Elizabeth raised the etching above her head, ready to smash it on the ground.

Anne didn't know if hearing "Mom" or "Seth" stopped Elizabeth, but Anne now saw her mother's face instead of the floor.

"You're my daughter?"

"Our daughter?" Matthew asked joining Elizabeth.

Anne began blurting out everything she remembered since she opened the box in the attic.

Elizabeth's shock turned to concern. "Stop," she insisted. "You've already said too much. If you say more, my future and your present could disappear. Leave before it's too late." She placed the etching face down on her workstation and left.

Anne pictured the dusty workstation and jumped out of the etching into present time. Everything would work out now that Mom knew when and where Seth attacked. Mom might even be downstairs waiting for her. Anne skipped down the steps to the bedroom — empty. Anne checked the time. Her trip lasted nearly an hour. Dinner, she decided. Everyone is probably in the dining hall. She pulled sweats over her bathing suit and rushed downstairs.

Anne stood in the dining hall doorway, looking for Mom. Simon who sat with some of the older students, waved. As Anne neared his table, Simon stood and took Anne aside. "Marcus is planning an all-out-attack on Seth's Ranch. Thomas is leading our animal response and he put me in charge of designing the insect attacks. Texas has a huge fire ant population, scorpions and cockroaches, too. I can promise you, Seth will wish he left you and your family alone."

Anne smiled weakly. Her plan had failed. Even with the warning, Seth captured Mom. Was Alex right? Did I make things worse? She pulled away from Simon and sat at an empty table, hoping he wouldn't follow her. She rested her head in her hands. What should I do now? She wondered.

"You really don't see me?" an excited voice asked from behind her.

As Anne looked up, Bakari stepped away from the wall. "Be honest," he said taking the seat next to her. "I'm just beginning my camouflage lessons."

"I think you mastered it already," Anne replied.

"Wood paneling is the easiest," he explained. "To past my test, I need to blend into twenty-two backgrounds — if Isadora even lets me test. She insisted I finish the basics of healing first. How am I going to become our best Assassin if she keeps slowing me down?" He flashed Anne a smile that lit up his face. "Can I join you for dinner?"

The abrupt change of subject caught Anne off guard. She thought she wanted to be alone in her misery, but found Bakari amusing. Unlike Simon who washed away her fears, Bakari raised questions in her mind. Anne selected mac-n-cheese and a salad, a sharp contrast to Bakari's spicy grilled fish and couscous. Midway through her meal and Bakari's review of his favorite poisons, George and Alex arrived.

The room burst into applause. Alex did it! He found the Key, Anne thought. But the cheers and back slaps were for George, not Alex.

"Well done." Simon shook George's hand. "But the next round won't be so easy. You have to get past me."

For a moment, George let his pride flood the room before containing it again.

"Let it all hang out. Sometimes emotions are meant to be shared," Simon said and glanced at Anne.

George and Alex filled their trays and joined Anne and Bakari. Alex dominated the conversation — rambling on about his Bruegel research and plans to channel the artist.

Bakari who practiced fading in and out of his chair suggested using Amazon leaf frog wax. "Some Amazon tribes used the secretion to boost their energy and mental focus," he explained.

"Does it work?" George asked.

"Not sure. I do know it makes you puke," Bakari said with disgust. "But there must be something to it. The drug companies have researched the wax for years. Some think it might cure cancers or Alzheimer's. I have a leaf frog in the Onyx lab."

"I'll pass," Alex said.

"What have you been up to?" George asked Anne.

She hesitated at bit too long. George stared at her suspiciously, and hot prickles climbed her spine. She glared at him and the sensation stopped. Anne straightened up in her chair. "Basic Transcender stuff," she lied. "Margaret wants me to sketch my dream about Mom. It might help find her."

"Your sketch would come alive with the right pigments," George said opening his CyberNexus. "Olivia's still in the pigment pavilion. I'll ask her to swipe some for you."

"I don't think I'm ready to create a living sketch," Anne said. What would happen if she messed up? Would Mom end up like Isadora's self-portrait?

"All the living-pigments are locked up, but Olivia can bring one that taps into your subconscious to enhance your memory." George explained and looked at his CyberNexus. "Olivia

III

can bring the powder, but she needs somewhere to mix the pigment."

"We can use Mom's lab," Alex suggested.

Anne hated the idea. Mom's lab was special to her now. She saw and spoke to Dad for the first time there, but she couldn't tell Alex she broke the time travel rules. They agreed to meet in the lab in thirty minutes. On her way out of the dining hall, Anne wrapped a handful of grapes in a napkin.

Olivia was the last to arrive. She stared wide-eyed at the supply cabinets and alchemy apparatus. When she reached Mom's workstation and saw the shelves of books, she squealed in delight. "I can't believe I'm really here," she said taking a deep breath as if perfume misted the air. "Your mom's the Collective's best Alchemist. May I look through her library?"

"Olivia, focus," George said rolling his eyes. "Pigments first — nasty boring research second."

"Who gave you a shot of confidence?" Olivia asked.

George smirked. "I aced my test."

"You really passed it!" Olivia shrieked; George blushed.

When Olivia calmed down, she sat at Mom's workstation and poured black powder onto a hand mirror. "Bone black," she said as she dripped walnut oil onto the pigment.

"Whose bones?" Bakari asked with morbid curiosity.

"Mostly charred dragons' teeth and claws," Olivia answered, mixing the oil and pigment with a palette knife. She presented the oil paint to Anne. "When you paint, think only about your dream — every detail you can remember."

George and Bakari watched Anne swish the paint with a fine-pointed brush. She turned and glared at them.

"Anne doesn't like an audience," Alex explained and ushered them to the far side of the room.

Anne waited until their murmuring stopped before beginning. The first brush strokes globbed paint unevenly onto the canvas. What's wrong with me? She put the black mess aside, and found a fresh canvas. She closed her eyes, reliving her dream. When she opened them, a collage of images covered the canvas: her Mom in the dingy tunnel, the ruins of the building and the fiery abyss with the oozing river. In the lower right corner, where translucent spiders mended their webs, the winged beast spun out of control and dropped Anne into the flames. "I'm coming inside, but I'm not visiting you," she told the monster.

Olivia rushed to Anne and grabbed her arm. "You can't go in until it's completely dry," she warned.

"Is that the monster who chased you?" Alex asked.

Anne cringed and nodded.

"Those look like energy spiders," George said.

"Then the winged demon must be a type of Plexian, too," Bakari surmised.

"Or one of their enemies," Anne suggested. "The spiders call it a curse."

Alex leaned close to the tunnel where Mom sat in misery. "What's that say on the wall?"

Anne squinted at the painting. "Where?"

"Behind the crate . . . It looks like 'ect Greek Island'."

"Does Seth have a base in the Mediterranean?" Olivia asked. "We should tell Marcus."

George typed a message on his CyberNexus. "Done." The CyberNexus chimed. "Marcus says not Greek bases, but he will get Bixia on it when she returns. Also, Uncle Wayne is waiting for Alex."

"Shoot! I forgot." Alex hurried down stairs and out of the room.

"I guess there's nothing more we can do until your painting dries," Olivia said. "See you in the morning."

Bakari lingered for a moment, looking expectantly at Anne, before following George and Olivia. Anne guessed he want to stay and talk, but she had one task left to complete, and she didn't want an audience. After brushing her teeth, Anne stood in front of Mom's dresser, a grape in one hand, the bracelet in the other. As she pictured Margaret's lake, water dripped on her head. On the ceiling, an eddy formed. She tossed a grape she saved from dinner inside the swirling water and watched it float to the lake's surface and bob in the gentle currents. "I did it! Aunt Margaret, did you get my present?" she asked, but heard no response.

Anne watched the eddy until it collapsed. She crawled into bed, hoping to dream of Mom and collect more details for her painting. Instead, she dreamed the painted Isadora broke into Lady Anne Brunel's painting through the bonfire hub. After a heated debate, Isadora convinced Lady Brunel to change the past and erase all evidence of the missing tablet pieces and the Primal Key. As they covered the paintings on Lady Brunel's wall with bone black, her world darkened. "I'll miss adventuring with Dumont d'Urville," Lady Brunel said, sadly, as she destroyed the painting commemorating the day the storm damaged the Carnelian Tablet.

CHAPTER ELEVEN

SHATTER POINT

Uncle Wayne worked with Alex late into the night, preparing him to channel Bruegel. He left Alex to ponder one critical question. Which Bruegel to channel — the calm stately guy or the disheveled painter? Alex, still in his jeans and t-shirt, lay on the bed studying the images on his CyberNexus. The composed Bruegel, well groomed with a long beard seemed fake — created for a formal occasion he would never want to attend. From his research, Alex learned Bruegel loved a joke. Bruegel also mocked The Church, exposed hypocrites and found peasants worthy subjects for fine art. But it was Dad's theories that swayed Alex the most. Dad filled an entire journal with evidence to support his theory (Bruegel was the first Amalgamator, a Transcender and an Alchemist). Any guy with that much talent must be half-crazy. Although Alex would rather navigate the calm man's soul, he decided Bruegel's true spirit was inside the eccentric painter.

Alex glanced at the clock — 2:13 a.m. With some luck, he could get five hours of sleep before the main event. He knew attempting to channel alone could leave him stuck inside Bruegel, so he asked Anne to tether him and George to monitor his progress. Alex slept soundly until Anne and George knocked on his bedroom door. He rolled out of bed and greeted his helpers. The syrup stains and grease on George's shirt told Alex waffles and bacon were on the breakfast menu. Alex's stomach grumbled, but food and channeling didn't mix. I'll pig-out later, he promised his stomach and sat on the floor.

"You're sure this is worth it?" Anne asked. "There's no way Bruegel saw the tablets."

"If Dad's right, Bruegel's mind holds more Plexian secrets than the tablets. I have to try."

George sat next to Alex. "So, what do I do?"

"Anne knows the drill. While she tethers me, I want you to tell her what I'm feeling and thinking. Don't worry if you sense I'm in danger or even in pain, but if I feel nothing —"

"You're being absorbed into Bruegel or dead," Anne said reaching for Alex's left hand. "Let's get this over with."

Alex nodded. He closed his eyes and stroked the silver ball with his thumb — searching for when the scruffy artist cared most about the ball. A foggy vision of Bruegel's life opened.

✠✠✠✠

Fear and exhilaration filled Bruegel as he firmly held the silver ball in his right hand. Beside a pile of paint brushes sat a chest with nine other balls of varying sizes — some ringed with jellyfish or viperfish, others crawling with spiders or ants. Bruegel consulted his notes on the spheres before selecting an ant-covered ball. As he approached *Kinderspiele*, Alex tried to release Bruegel's mind, but it was too late.

"Time to enter a new world," Bruegel said and jumped into his painting.

As Bruegel and Alex arrived, a girl selling brick powder announced, "Make way for the Master." Her message rippled from game to game up the street until gradually, the games stopped. The children opened a path for the artist. Some kids bowed, others gawked as Bruegel passed the town hall and turned down the alleyway. The narrow dirt road extended across a bridge and disappeared over a hill into the countryside. Bruegel placed the ant-covered ball on the ground and waited — nothing. He nudged it with his foot. Several children crowded around looking at the ball and then back to Bruegel. A boy pulled a stone marble from his leather pouch. He kneeled and flicked the shooter at the ball — clink. The ball split, spewing translucent ants into the alleyway. The ants tunneled into the dirt and within seconds, a sinkhole formed, sending tremors through *Kinderspiele*. More of the alleyway disappeared. Three kids toppled toward the hole. As their friends tried to pull them to safety, Bruegel staggered backward, against the town hall. The hole swirled and grew. From its depths hundreds of bat-like demons with blood-red eyes shot into the air.

"What have I done?" Bruegel yelled, watching the demons soar up the street, scattering screaming kids as they made their way to the cathedral. In an attempt to stabilize the breach, Bruegel threw the jellyfish ball toward the hole. It impacted near the rim.

"Forgive me, children. I have opened the gates of Hell!" He ran down the street to the girl selling brick dust and touched her head gently. "I will repair your world," he promised and disappeared.

Back in his studio, he rifled through his desk looking for the right key. Alex recognized the key's bit — it was Grandpa's Carnelian Tablet crazy key. As Bruegel locked the chest of spheres, the key broke and Alex's reality shattered. Like a hammer striking a window, his world fractured. Each crack showed a possible future — not Bruegel's, but the spheres'.

Thousands of lines flashed from the shatter point. The short fractures, only minutes long, ended with explosions. In a slightly longer line, a man in red tights and cloak displayed a sphere hovering over his hand. More fracture lines opened. Alex saw Dad standing in front of *Kinderspiele*, clutching the jellyfish ball. "I'm sorry, Bridget," he said.

The ant-covered ball on Isadora's bookcase flashed by, as did Seth, clutching Bruegel's notes on constructing spheres.

Five longer fractures opened, racing forward for centuries. In the longest, Mom and Lamia struggled over a gun in a long, grimy hallway. Mom wrested the gun from Lamia, but Lamia planted a sidekick on Mom's arm. The gun flew across the room clanking as it hit the stone floor. They both dashed to reach the weapon, but Lamia reached it first.

"You can't escape." Lamia taunted her.

Mom backed up, hands raised.

The gun still trained on Mom, Lamia reached for a bag on the floor, pulling out one of Bruegel's worm-covered spheres. "It's time you became a permanent part of the past." As she placed the sphere on the floor, the metal worms glowed and slithered around the ball. "In twelve hours Seth will either reach the higher dimensions or fail — again. Either way, your fate is sealed."

"Seth needs me alive," Mom challenged.

"Not any more. Isadora's a fool to think she can stop us. Soon we'll have the Primal Key and Anne. I'm sure we can persuade your daughter to share the Collective's secrets."

"No!" Mom lunged at Lamia.

As the gun went off, Alex flew back in time, the fractures reversed direction sending time-shards toward the center of the fracture point — Alex. One-by-one, the shards pierced his body until the pain reached an unspeakable level. His senses overloaded.

✠✠✠✠✠

"Alex!" Anne yanked the silver ball from his hand.

Alex curled his knees to his chest. He didn't say anything until the deep, piercing pain diminished and the glass shards in his skin felt like bee stings. He stretched out on his back, staring at the ceiling.

Anne clutched Alex's hand. "George said you died. I had to pull you back."

Alex closed his eyes trying to piece together what he had seen. "Seth is using Bruegel's spheres to rip time. Lamia's going to shoot mom. There were ten balls at first. Bruegel didn't have the tablets but he had Grandpa's key." He stopped his eyes wide and looked at Anne. "I saw what Bruegel unleashed in the alleyway — hundreds of your monsters."

Anne helped him sit, then leaned him against the bed next to George.

"Pretty intense pain. Hope it was worth it," George said, wiping sweat from his face. "Do me a favor. Next time you go diving into someone's soul ask Simon not me to help."

Alex wanted to quip back, but didn't have the energy. As his bee stings reduced to pin pricks, his stomach settled. "Let me get this out in one shot before I forget the details." He took a deep breath and recounted everything he could remember.

"Are you sure Lamia killed Mom?" Anne asked.

Alex took a moment to think before shaking his head. "No, but if we don't find her before the sphere rips time Mom will die"

"My painting will be dry tonight. We'll find a clue inside it," Anne said.

"Then what?" George asked, letting his doubt flood the room. "You and Anne run off to save your Mom and run right into Seth's hands? He captures Anne and the sphere still explodes. Great plan! I didn't hear you mention any 'happily ever after' futures in the time fractures. Marcus is —"

"I didn't see Marcus swooping in to save Mom either," Alex said gruffly.

Anne slapped the floor with her hand making Alex and George flinch. "I don't care what you did or didn't see. I refuse to believe the future is set. If we can't change the future from here, maybe we should try erasing part of the past . . ." Anne eyes opened wide. "That's what Isadora is planning." She stood and ran from the room.

Alex and George exchanged a concerned look. "We better go after her," George said.

They caught up to Anne in the courtyard outside the mansion. Alex grabbed her arm. "Tell me what's wrong?"

"No time. It might already be too late." She pulled free and ran down the steps into the garden.

"Anne wait!" Alex called after her. Confused, he turned to George.

George shrugged and took off after Anne.

They found Anne in the meditation room standing in front of Isadora's self-portrait and then she disappeared.

"Can you follow her?" Alex asked, although he knew George hated using his Transcender talents.

"Not a chance! The real Isadora is bad enough —"

Before Alex could argue with George, Anne popped back next to them.

"Isadora's gone!" She strode over to Lady Brunel's portrait.

"You can't go in there," George insisted. "Even Bixia won't visit Lady Brunel. The older paintings are unstable."

"I have to go," Anne insisted. "It might be our only chance to see the Carnelian Tablet."

"Then I'm going with you." Alex grabbed her arm. She jumped, dragging him with her.

LADY BRUNEL'S "THE CHEVRETTE."

CHAPTER TWELVE

THE CHEVRETTE

Layers of colorful cobwebs ripped as Anne pulled Alex through the oil paint.

"Isadora?" Lady Brunel asked. "Did you bring the bone black pigment?"

"It's Anne, her granddaughter."

"How wonderful! It has been eons since someone new visited me. Are you here to help save Elizabeth?"

Alex noticed Lady Brunel looked slightly to the right of them. "I'm over here," he said, waving his arms.

"Ah, you brought the Amalgamator. I understand my ghost has called on Alex a few times. Have you found the missing symbols yet? Well, soon that won't matter."

"You can't see us, can you?" Alex asked.

"No, extended sight is a luxury for the newer paintings. I only see what my granddaughter, Margaret, painted."

"You can't destroy your paintings," Anne insisted.

"I must. Isadora explained everything. Seth captured Elizabeth and now he wants the Primal Key. If I destroy my knowledge of the Carnelian Tablet and of that nasty bat who told me to connect them, then Elizabeth won't know about the Key to begin with. Maybe she'll come home and improve my painting."

"She's not the real Isadora," Anne said. "It was her self-portrait."

"Nonsense. My fire died out years ago. When the pigment aged it lost its luster. The only way into my painting is from the physical world."

Anne glared at Lady Brunel. Alex recognized her expression. She was calculating how best to manipulate the situation.

"I wondered," Anne began, "the paintings on your wall, Where are the originals?"

"Destroyed — burned in a studio fire. Margaret tried to save them but, sadly, she was too late. What a pity. They were my best. Fortunately Margaret painted my portrait before the fire." Lady Brunel happily waved her arm past her wall of paintings. "Most of Dumont's memories are intact."

"There are living paintings inside your living painting?" Alex asked.

Lady Brunel's spirits soared. "Of course! I invented our pigment techniques. I would go mad if I didn't have places to visit occasionally. Isadora promised we will only destroy *Surviving the Surge* and *The Plexian's Plot*."

"Could we visit *Surviving the Surge*? One last time — before it's gone forever?" Anne asked.

"What an excellent idea! It's been so long since someone accompanied me on a Dumont adventure. Your grandfather loved visiting Antarctica. One time he fell off the boat, and we lost him for hours. Luckily, he came prepared for the elements. We should start with something less dangerous — the Greek archipelago. The water is a beautiful blue and the food . . . well, there is nothing like it anywhere else in the world!"

Alex edged close to Anne and whispered, "What's your plan?"

Anne pointed to the painting of a three-mast ship rolled onto its side. A large, cresting wave flooded the deck. "Is it possible to see how the Carnelian Tablet was damaged? We can visit the other paintings another time."

"Yes, please," Alex said, unable to hide his excitement. Dumont d'Urville topped Isadora's list of people to channel. Uncle Wayne had tried for years to find his ghost. Eventually, he gave up. Apparently Dumont passed peacefully to the other side despite his tragic death. All this time, his memory of the Carnelian Tablet lay hidden in Lady Brunel's world.

"I will take you one time. You will survive if you follow my instructions — exactly. I can go in myself, but Anne, you will need to guide Alex. Picture yourself next to the mast nearest that hatch. It leads below deck."

Anne landed Alex gently on the boat, but Alex immediately fell to his knees. The wind and rain pelted his face as the ship rolled to one side. Men, anchored with ropes, attempted to right the vessel. Anne leaned against the mast, next to Lady Brunel. With a jolt, the ship rocked back in the other direction. Alex slid on his stomach as another wave crested over the ship. The rush of water washed them below deck.

Lady Brunel sat on the floor, wringing water from her hair. "After 109 years, you would think I could find a better way to get in here."

Anne tried to stand, but the boat rocked, sliding her into the wall. "Can we get on with this?" she pleaded.

Lady Brunel led them through a hatch into the ship's hold. "We must hurry. The Captain is about to make his turn. That is when the tablet breaks."

Alex was the first one down the ladder. Feeling the ship shudder in a new direction, he steadied himself against the base of a mast. Dumont was securing the Carnelian Tablet in the ship's hold. Before leaving, he pulled a cloth off the tablet and rolled it up tightly. He glanced at the tablet one last time before hurrying up the ladder.

Alex tumbled toward the tablet. He knelt down and touched the bottom corner. "It's undamaged, but the symbols don't make sense! It's covered in scribbles!" he yelled over the roaring waves pummeling the bulkhead.

"Grab onto something," Lady Brunel cautioned. "The Captain is turning into the waves to keep the boat from capsizing."

The side-to-side rocking stopped and the bow quickly rose. When Alex feared the boat might flip, it crashed down the other side of the wave. A cask broke free of its ties and landed on the tablet, breaking the corner. The boat tossed again, sending the broken pieces skittering across the hold. Alex lunged, grabbing the largest piece as the ship crashed down another wave. Sprawled on the floor, he carefully examined his prize.

"It's blank! What happened?" he asked, turning it over-and-over in disbelief.

"I think we should go," Lady Brunel suggested. "In a few moments, things get much worse. Anne, grab Alex and picture yourself back in my painting."

As Anne reached Alex, the ship rose almost ninety degrees. Anne quickly popped them back into Lady Brunel's portrait.

"I don't understand! The symbols were gibberish, and then they disappeared," Alex yelled, his voice booming without the storm's blustering. He kept looking at his hands, but the tablet corner was gone.

"You thought you could see the whole tablet? You are not the first. The cast damaged the tablet before Dumont translated the symbols. The few details you saw surfaced when I painted his adventure. With my pigments, I liberated memories he buried in his subconscious. The tablet remains blank unless he looks directly at it. Even then, the symbols distort. Where shall we go next? Would you like to visit *The Plexian's Plot* before I destroy it? There is not much to see . . . only the tricky Bat sending me on a fool's errand."

"That's my Bat," Alex whispered.

Lady Brunel abruptly turned. Even though Alex knew she was blind, he stared right at him. "The Bat claimed the greatest Amalgamator would trigger death and destruction if I didn't find the Primal Key. Alex, you're not a villain — are you?" she asked.

"Of course not," Anne answered for him. She looked at the enormous bat, beating its wings over a cowering Lady Brunel. "I think we should go."

"Will you return soon? I get so lonely." Lady Brunel asked. "Dumont's memory of New Zealand is wonderfully vivid."

Anne promised to return for another adventure before jumping back to the meditation room.

"What happened?" George asked. "You've been gone more than an hour! I was about to go get Isadora."

Anne explained her failed plan to save Lady Brunel's world and to see the Carnelian Tablet. "I've got to let Margaret know what's happening. Maybe she can stop Isadora." Anne disappeared into Margaret's painting.

George's face brightened. "Do you think some of the stuff from the ship made it to a nautical museum? Maybe the tablet pieces are in archives or even on exhibit."

"George, that's brilliant," Alex said and reached for his CyberNexus to begin a search. After a few moments, Alex tossed the device on the table in frustration. "Tons of hits about the *Venus de Milo*, but nothing about the *Chevrette*."

"Maybe it's with Venus in The Louvre. The transportation center has direct links to most friendly museums."

Anne popped back into the meditation room, startling George. "Margaret doesn't know how Isadora is traveling between paintings, but she will try to stop her. She also wants me to send her a mango. Where am I going to get a mango?"

"Paris?" George suggested.

"We're going to The Louvre," Alex said.

"Exactly how are you planning to get there?"

"The transportation center — we're hitching a ride with my favorite Transcender," Alex smiled at Anne.

As George led the way through the Agate wing down to the

transportation center, Anne tried to poke holes in Alex's plan. "You don't even know where to look in The Louvre — it's huge. Besides, SANDY will never let us go."

"She won't notice until we're gone," George replied.

"Gone where?" Chasca asked as stepping out of the transportation center's deep shadows.

"Paris, want to come?" Alex offered.

"I'm still grounded," Chasca pouted. "I'd blow your cover. Until tomorrow, any portals within five feet of me shut down."

"Then why are you down here?" Anne asked, an edge of suspicion in her voice.

Chasca smiled smugly at Anne. "All the masters are busy preparing to attack Seth. No one's using the portals so I'm studying for my level-four test. Isadora selects ten random destinations. I have to find each portal, make the jump, and return with a detailed description of what I saw."

"That shouldn't be hard," Anne said, wandering into the transportation center, "I mean, for someone with your talents."

Chasca glared at Anne. "The hardest part comes after the ten trips. You see, the portals are laid out in a spiral, but somewhere in there is a hidden door. I have to traverse the corkscrew and locate it by feeling the anomaly."

"I'll help you study later," Alex offered.

"Don't move," Chasca warned Anne. "You're surrounded by portals."

"I know. These three go to museums, and this one connects to a military bunker. Ah, here's The Louvre."

"How could you possibly know that without the map," Chasca challenged.

Anne grinned, dangling the bracelet from her forefinger. "It lets me see through portals." She sidestepped the portals until she stood in the middle of the room. "Chasca, where does this one lead? All I can see is darkness on the other side."

"That spot's reserved. Isadora's saving it for something special," Chasca replied.

Lights flickered through the halls leading away from the transportation center then faded. Lightning bolts erupted from the portal.

Alex dropped to the floor. "Anne, what have you done?"

"Intruders in the transportation center," SANDY reported. "Massive energy —" SANDY's voice fizzled then failed.

CHAPTER THIRTEEN

*K

SPIDERS IN AKKAD

Energy spiders gushed from the portal. Their bodies — rippling irregular rings — pulsated and twisted. Legs flashing, they circled about Anne and spun a tightly woven web surrounding the black hole. The spiders wrapped her in fluorescing webs, pulling her toward the dark portal. Anne struggled, but the webbing clung tight to her skin. Alex lunged to save Anne, but was too late. With a flash, Anne disappeared into the portal.

She landed on something hard and toppled onto a rough, dusty floor. A searing pain shot up her side. She checked her shirt for blood. Nothing punctured or broken, she decided — just bruises. She gently flexed her arm and tested her ankle before attempting to stand. In the dim light cast by the energy spiders, she saw the three-foot-tall gold boulder that broke her fall and almost cracked her ribs. It sat atop a stone box at least seven feet long. Not a box — a sarcophagus, Anne realized. I'm in a tomb.

An energy spider suspended from a thread of light dangled above the boulder. "Take it. Stop the curse."

Anne tried to push the boulder off the sarcophagus. It wouldn't budge. Wrapping her arms around it, she heaved. The pain in her side spiked. She cried out and stumbled backward. Strings of light wrapped Anne in a crackling web, catching her before she fell into a hole in the corner of the tomb. For a moment, she teetered on the edge before the spiders tugged her back to the sarcophagus.

"The boulder's too heavy!" Anne called to the spiders. More strings of light wrapped around Anne and the boulder, snatching her, painfully, over the sarcophagus and back through the portal. As she landed on the transportation center floor, the boulder's surface sizzled with energy shocking Anne and dissolving the webs. When the last spiders departed, the lights in the Tablet Complex flickered on.

Alex paled at the sight of Anne's dusty clothing, smudged face, and frazzled hair. "What did they do to you?"

"Those were the spiders from my dream," Anne explained. "They wanted me to find that thing."

"It's a golden dodecahedron," Chasca said in awe.

"A what?" Alex asked.

Chasca inched closer to the gold ball. "Twelve pentagons connected like a sphere. I wonder what all those lines and triangles mean."

Alex helped Anne stand. She was glad he held her left arm because a bruise the size of an apple was growing on her right.

"What's going on down here?" Isadora demanded, striding into the room with Abigail in tow. "The entire complex blacked out and SANDY's disabled."

Abigail gasped. "Anne, you look awful!" She dug in her purse, pulled out wet-wipes and tried to clean the grime from Anne's face. That's right, Anne silently seethed, my face not my bruised ribs are top priority.

"Plexian energy spiders threw her through a portal. The trip was rough, but she's okay. Right?" Alex gave Anne a worried look.

Anne felt like a bull had trampled her, but forced a smile while Abigail moved from face cleaning to hair styling in an attempt to make her look presentable.

"The spiders gave Anne this," George said, stepping away from the dodecahedron.

Isadora rushed to examine the artifact. "This is Akkadian."

Abigail abandoned the clean-up-Anne-project and joined Isadora. "I'll contact Emma. She's the best with Akkadian."

Alex pulled Anne aside. "Don't go near that thing," he insisted. "When you get near the dodecahedron, you change. I don't know who you become or from when, but one of your past lives is directly linked to that thing."

"But it's meant for me." Anne's anger started to swell. Couldn't Alex see? The spiders took her — only her — to find it."

Alex let out a frustrated huff. "I know that dodecahedron is for you. I've never felt more certain about anything, but until we understand it, be extremely careful."

Anne turned toward the dodecahedron. Isadora was attempting to translate the Akkadian. Somehow, Anne knew every word without looking.

"This key symbol means 'to exist.'" Isadora said decisively.

The symbol ⟦ ⟧ flashed into Anne's mind.

Isadora tapped the dodecahedron. "And the one on the top says 'to lead.'"

No," Anne whispered. "The symbol ⟦ ⟧ means 'the leader who walks in front,' and the next ⟦ ⟧ means 'to give.'"

"I'm not sure what this symbol ⟦ ⟧ represents," Isadora said.

"To enter heaven," Anne said more forcefully, but Isadora and Abigail didn't hear her. Alex and George, however, gave her their full attention.

Anne recited, "The symbol ⟦ ⟧ means to proclaim, ⟦ ⟧ is to know and ⟦ ⟧ means to kill."

Anne shouted, "The next four are ⟦ ⟧ accept, ⟦ ⟧ return, ⟦ ⟧ bind and ⟦ ⟧ prevent."

"Stop!" George warned as Anne approached the dodecahedron.

"The symbol ⟦ ⟧ on the bottom tells me how to survive."

"Anne, you're changing again. Who are you?" Alex asked.

"I am Enheduanna, High Priestess of Nanna, the moon god!" Anne proclaimed, raising her hands high above her head. The dodecahedron glowed. Anne collapsed.

CHAPTER FOURTEEN

VISION QUEST

Alex sat next to Anne's hospital bed feeling helpless. Chasca rested her hand on his arm. "She'll be okay. The trip to get that dodecahedron must have overwhelmed her."

"They don't even know what happened to her." Alex flipped his hand toward the hallway where Isadora and Aunt Helena discussed possible treatments for Anne's injuries, while Aunt Abigail stood silently near the door staring at Anne.

"Anne's tougher than you think," George said.

Alex stared at the angry blisters on Anne's neck and face. "She shouldn't have to be, and Helena has no idea what caused those burns. They're getting bigger and spreading."

Helena had asked Bakari, who excelled at identifying poisons, to monitor Anne. He studied the blisters. "You said the dodecahedron caused them?"

"Must be," George said. "It happened when she translated those symbols. Who did Anne say she was before passing out?"

"Enheduanna," Chasca replied.

George typed the name into his CyberNexus. He whistled softly. "She was a princess, a priestess, and an author. In fact, she was the first author known by name."

Bakari peered over George's arm to see the screen. "It says here she was born in 2285 BCE and was the daughter of Sargon of Akkad. She was high priestess of the moon god, Nanna. So she's definitely qualified to read the symbols on the dodecahedron."

"Emma believes the dodecahedron is the Primal Key," Abigail said approaching Anne's bed. "She found bat-like glyphs flying around its equator that match the symbols on the gemstone tablets. Such a shame the relic over-whelmed Anne."

Alex knew what Abigail meant. She wasn't sorry for Anne's injuries; she was annoyed Anne couldn't help with the translation. Alex couldn't find the right words to respond, but George did.

"You finally have the Primal Key. Here's betting you're not paying Aunt Elizabeth's ransom, are you?"

"That's not my decision, but caving to Seth's demands won't help," Abigail explained, as if telling a young child why giving his lunch money to the class bully only made matters worse. "Seth will keep Elizabeth hostage as long as it serves his needs."

"You must do something!" Alex demanded.

"We have," Isadora said, joining them. "Marcus and Bixia are planning our response, and I recalled the Collective to help them. Leave Elizabeth's rescue in their capable hands. Focus your energies on finding the bottom of the Carnelian Tablet. We won't know if the dodecahedron is the Primal Key until the tablets are fully connected. Imagine — we might finally unlock the mysteries of the Plexus."

Chasca picked up George's CyberNexus and reread the entry. "If the dodecahedron connects the tablets, maybe Enheduanna knew something about the others, like what was written on the Carnelian Tablet."

Even if Enheduanna knew something, Alex didn't like the idea of an ancient priestess taking over Anne's body. Anne needed to heal, not answer a bunch of questions. "The Carnelian Tablet was written in Linear B a thousand years after Enheduanna died."

"Want to try The Louvre?" George suggested.

"To look for the tablet pieces?" Isadora looked incensed. "Why do you think Collective masters manage the great museums? We've thoroughly searched them and manage new acquisitions."

"Then what else do you suggest?" Alex asked throwing his hands into the air. Isadora only cared about her stupid tablets and finding a way into the Plexus — not saving Mom. If the futures Alex saw in the shatter point came to pass, Mom would die, Seth would capture Anne and the Primal Key. I must change that future! Alex pushed out of the chair hard enough that it hit the wall. "I'm sick of talking to dead people and channeling past lives. Find the tablet yourself!" He stormed out of the room.

"Wait," Bakari called, following Alex out the medical center's front door. Alex continued down the sidewalk, but at a pace that allowed Bakari to catch up. "Cosmo the Frog offers up her very best," he said, handing Alex a vile. "I nipped it from the lab."

Alex looked at the goo, scrunching up his nose. "What's in it?"

"Amazon leaf frog wax. It might help you focus. You know, if you want to try channeling again."

Alex nodded and pocketed the vile.

"I'll stay with Anne," Bakari promised. "I'll call you if her condition changes."

Bakari turned back toward the Medical Center. Alex knew he was trying to help, but wanted to be alone. Alex reached the Estate's main road and followed it toward the mountain — away from Isadora and the Tablet Complex. The late afternoon sun warmed his skin, while light breezes took the edge off the heat. Everything looked vibrant, but Alex felt miserable. He had no clue how to change the future and save Mom. Even worse, if he chose the wrong path he could make things worse. He followed a sign pointing toward "Ghost Lake." The road ended where a dock jutted fifteen feet into the lake. The boards creaked and the dock swayed as he made his way to the end where he found a pile of stones.

He picked up the largest rock and hurled it into the water. After a satisfying "plunk," the stone was gone, but the countless circular ripples rolled on and on. He searched through the stones looking for the best skipper — smooth, round and just the right weight for a fast spin. He curled his finger around the stone, cocked his arm and skipped the stone across the water. Seven skips, not shabby, but he could do better. Alex sorted the remaining stones on the dock into two piles — skippers and plunkers. Nine tosses later he achieved a personal best of nineteen skips. He grabbed the plunkers and threw them as high as he could. They rained down, "plopping," as they hit the surface. Alex watched their circular waves overlap. If only rippling a change into the future was as simple as selecting the right stones.

He reached into his pocket and clutched the vial of frog goo. Everything else had failed to give him the answers. Maybe Bakari's shaman mind-altering drug was worth a shot, even if it made him puke his guts out. As he pulled the vial from his pocket, a hawk landed on a dead tree jutting out of the lake and screeched.

"What do you want?" Alex asked.

The hawk took flight, crying "kee-aah," as it circled above Alex. Then it swooped to the surface of the lake and vanished.

Did that thing kill itself? Alex pushed through brambles and scrambled over boulders to reach where the hawk disappeared. A single feather floated near the shore. Alex carefully picked it up. The hawk screeched again startling Alex. He lost his balance and face planted into the lake. He slopped to shore and wiped his muddy hands on his jeans.

"Where are you . . . you mangy bird?" he asked, picking up a stone. "I'm going to clock you." He heard the hawk's soft "kee" above him. From piles of dry sticks on the crown of the tree, the hawk gazed down at him. Alex dropped his rock. This was her territory — he was trespassing. "You wouldn't happen to know a better path out of here, would you?" Alex asked, picking wet leaves out of his hair. To his surprise, the hawk left her nest.

Alex scrambled up a steep slope to a wide rock shelf in front of a cave. The hawk circled above him. Alex plopped down on a rock near the mouth of the cave and glared at the bird. "If you think I'm going in there, you're sadly mistaken. Caves aren't my thing."

The hawk landed in her nest and preened her feathers, biding her time. As Alex watched her, he began to feel the presence of others who had sat on this rock — hunters stopping to rest and travelers seeking safety for the night. A sense of calm displaced the anxieties he bottled up since Seth's attack. Drawn to a feeling that something greater lived inside, he took a few steps toward the cave where the shadows overtook the gray and brown rock. "Hello. Is anyone — or thing — in there?"

Silence.

The jagged rock cave roof sloped down quickly. Alex hunched down and inched his way toward a dark triangular hole. Holding his breath and praying the walls wouldn't collapse, he crawled inside. Darkness shrouded all but the sunlit mouth of the cave. He slid his hand up the wall until he was standing.

"Okay, I've made it this far without passing out. Please make this worthwhile." Keeping his hand on the wall, he inched forward. Occasionally he stopped, listened for movement then he gathered the courage to move deeper. To his relief the cave was small — no more than fifteen feet deep. In less than ten minutes — although to Alex it seemed an eternity — he reached the exit. "All that for nothing?" he grumbled and ducked his head to leave. A small brown bat flapped past his ear. Alex jumped and whacked his head against the jagged ceiling. His vision blurred, as he staggered to the wall. In rhythm to the pounding in his head, he heard the Bat's raspy whisper:

To find your answers look within your clan.
Bring back the past. Channel Mistress Anne.
A shaman you have been before.
In this life you must be more.
Traverse her past and chart
The places where you start
To see her transform
and stop the storm.
To make the leap
Fall deep
Asleep.

Alex held his aching head. "Thanks a lot, Bat." Falling asleep was tempting, but time was running out for Mom and — if he was right — Anne. He searched for the cave's mouth, but the triangle of light was gone. "Great!" Alex said angrily. "So, you want me to channel Lady Anne Brunel — again. Fine, but it won't help." He leaned back against the wall, took a deep calming breath, and pictured Lady Anne.

Lady Brunel arrived immediately. Her energy lit up the cave casting deep shadows. "My, you have grown. Not an inviting place for a conversation, though. Where are we?"

"In a cave on the Collective's estate," Alex replied.

"Wonderful! Then I am sure you visited my portrait. I was reluctant to be blind and cooped up in two dimensions for the rest of eternity, but once my granddaughter, Margaret, discovered a way to provide me with a few diversions, I agreed. How am I faring?"

Alex didn't want to tell her how Lady Brunel had practically begged them to visit her again. The real Lady Brunel wouldn't approve. "I think you — I mean, she — gets a little bored. She can see inside her painted adventures. They keep her —"

"Sane? Well, at least I am not completely blind as a bat." Lady Brunel seemed pleased.

"Actually, bats can see . . . . The Bat . . . yes . . . that's why I need to speak with you."

Lady Brunel looked startled. "The Bat? It spoke to you?"

"He told me to 'Channel Mistress Anne.'"

"That Bat is full of riddles." She huffed. "I am sorry. I have no answers for you, but I do not believe the Bat sent you on a fool's errand. What else did he say?" Lady Anne took a seat on the cave floor, and Alex recited the message. Her face brightened, illuminating the edges of the cave. "How exciting, the answers must be hidden within my past lives. Have you traversed them?"

Alex had tried, but entering his ancestors' past lives was tricky. His silence gave him away.

"I tried every family member, but when I go even one life back, I feel I'm trespassing or messing up someone's future — or my own." Alex cringed, remembering his trip in Aunt Margaret's lives. He had landed in the 1400s in the middle of a trial determining her witchy status. Sensing his arrival, Margaret panicked. Her confusion sealed her fate. Later they burned her at the stake.

"What if I give you permission to trespass? Just promise me one thing. If I do anything embarrassing, please keep it to yourself." She winked and rose to leave.

Maybe her consent would make it easier this time, Alex thought.

"Soon you will become the Amalgamator," Lady Anne said, her ghost form fading. "Proceed with caution. Many great people with good intentions have triggered death and destruction."

"Thanks for the pep talk," Alex muttered and prepared to traverse Lady Anne's lives. He opened himself to time and chanted her name. For what seemed like hours, he tried and failed to enter any of her lives. Exhausted, he drifted asleep. He dreamed that purple and blue orbs grew on the floor like mushrooms. The mushrooms glowed and, with a soft phffft, split open. Instead of fungus spores, thousands of wispy bats emerged. They whizzed about the cave and then collided, forming a single translucent bat. It sang:

> When our great lords denied permission
> For me to change my family's mission,
> I chose to break Plexian tradition
> And left you to your own volition.

"What Plexian tradition?" Alex asked. The Bat answered with a blinding flash. Alex felt his reality shatter for the second time that day, this time, instead of futures, the center of the shatter pointed back four thousand years. A single fracture line stretched before him. "Where am I?" Alex asked the Bat.

The Bat sang on:

> This is the first time you two coexist,
> You died at birth and did not assist
> With my desperate plan for her to resist
> The terrible curse that swells in our midst.

"I never died as a baby," Alex insisted. His first life had been in Athens and he had lived for fifty-three years. "Who is the girl I didn't help? Is this Lady Anne's first life? And what is the curse?"

The Bat flitted an airborne somersault, trailing strings of light in its wake.

> You must help her to make the transition.
> I'll show you the bits you missed,
> But to safeguard her future I must insist
> That your body remains an apparition.

The Bat imploded, leaving the ghostly Alex stranded in the past.

CHAPTER FIFTEEN

MISTRESS ANNE'S 36 LIVES

With nowhere else to go, Alex's ghost floated into the fracture line. He watched the birth of a princess who would become the high priestess, Enheduanna. There must be a mistake, he thought. This is his sister's past life, not Lady Brunel's. He tried to release his mind and body back to the cave; instead, he landed in a different part of Enheduanna's life.

Enheduanna, now a young woman, dressed in a flowing red-and-gold dress, went about her duties: recording the moon, performing rituals and writing hymns. Occasionally, in secret, she worked on the dodecahedron. For hours, Alex watched her write on gold foil sheets before attaching them to the dodecahedron. He tried to read the Akkadian, but the instant she finished a symbol it distorted. A week after Enheduanna's thirty-fifth birthday, she completed the dodecahedron.

"Take it to the temple of Nigel," Enheduanna told her attendants. "Place it in the cella, the small chamber, at the base of the moon goddess's statue."

At nightfall, Alex followed Enheduanna into the temple of Nigel. They wound through rooms until they reached the temple's heart where the goddess lived. Enheduanna climbed the stairs to the base of the statue. From the folds of her robes, she withdrew a pentagon-shaped golden bracelet marked with five symbols. When she slipped it onto her wrist, the dodecahedron glowed. In her other hand, she held a silver ball.

"That's Bruegel's jellyfish ball!" Alex exclaimed.

Lightning cracked around the room as Enheduanna placed her hand on the dodecahedron. The top split. Inside, Alex saw a huge maw filled with thousands of spear-like teeth. It belched, and hundreds of fluorescent jellyfish spewed out. In seconds, the first jellyfish reached the edge of the dodecahedron. Its tentacles sloshed into the temple.

"Demagogue," its voice thundered, "Your earth must perish to break the curse."

Its tentacles slashed against Enheduanna's neck. She screamed, but did not pull back. Instead, she squeezed the little ball against the creature and sang her exaltation of Inanna. She prayed for Inanna to rain fire upon the creatures and to endow her with strength to protect her nation. The tentacles dissolved. Enheduanna, collapsed, unconscious. Alex watched as the maw inhaled, sucking the other jellyfish down its gullet. When the maw closed, the winged beast that had attacked Anne hovered near the edge of the dodecahedron.

Its voice sizzled as it spoke — a voice Alex recognized as the Bat's.

> Time and again you will succumb.
> Until perfected your skills become.
> Then the Demagogue shall arise
> And return the Key or cause your demise.

The dodecahedron closed, sealing the Plexus. Alex approached Enheduanna. Her body heaved for breath. Ribbons of blisters marred her face and neck in a pattern identical to Anne's wounds. Alex sat helplessly next to her for hours until she died. Shortly before dawn, Enheduanna's attendants found her body. At her funeral, her brother, Manishtusu, the King, recounted her great deeds. This woman was the key to uniting the Sumerian and Akkadian gods. She brought peace and stability everywhere she went. Without her, the empire would have collapsed in chaos. They buried her body in a tomb beneath the temple and placed the dodecahedron atop her sarcophagus.

Alone, Alex sat in the tomb and waited. Now what? He felt in his pocket for the vial, wondering if it would help get him home.

A frog jumped from behind the dodecahedron. It looked at Alex and chirped.

"How did you get in here? You wouldn't be related to Cosmo the leaf frog — would you?" Alex reached for the frog.

To his utter surprise, his hand didn't pass through it. This frog was the first thing he had touched since he arrived in Enheduanna's life. It was cold and then wet. "Yuck! Frog pee!" he said, dropping the frog.

It chirped again. Another frog leapt out from behind a bowl, then several others from the other side of Enheduanna's coffin. Soon the floor was hopping with frogs. Alex pressed up against the sarcophagus to avoid squashing them. Behind him, the sarcophagus's top shifted, scraping stone against stone. The lid toppled to the floor, and frogs tumbled over the edge. In seconds, the frogs buried Alex's feet and ankles. Under the weight of the frogs, the floor cracked then collapsed. Alex and the frogs fell through a cavern and into an underground river. The cold current dragged him along the rough cave wall. In the distance he heard the water roar. Although it was too dark to see, he knew what was coming and desperately swam upstream, but the strong current swept him over a waterfall.

As he fell, a single scene repeated in his mind. He watched Henhenet, the maniacal priestess from The Met, die while giving birth. Her child would have died, too, but the goddess Hathor appeared and took the child into her body. When Alex finally landed, it was not with a large splash in a pool, but with a thud that knocked the air from his lungs. Slowly, he regained his breath. A few surviving frogs jumped down a tunnel. From the opposite direction, Alex heard voices. Unsure whom he would find, he cautiously crept down the long, musty hall.

A girl yelled. "The gate vanished! What do we do? We have to find a way out, or the Minotaur will eat us!"

"We will find a way to escape!" a boy replied.

Then Alex heard a voice that made his heart ache. It was his daughter, Airlea, from his life in ancient Greece.

"Damianos, you know only Daedalus knows the way out of his Labyrinth," Airlea said. Alex heard no fear in her voice. She sounded relieved. Desperate to reach her, he ran toward her voice.

"We have to try," Damianos said.

"I will attract the Minotaur. It could give you enough time to find a way out," Airlea said. "Take the others in the opposite direction."

Damianos kissed Airlea's cheek. "If I survive, I promise you will be remembered as a great hero. If we die, I'll see you in Elysium. You have earned a labor-free afterlife."

Airlea split from the group. "Airlea, stop!" Alex yelled, running after her. His daughter could not hear him. She sang and skipped through the Labyrinth. Alex followed as she wound through passageways. Loud screams echoed from behind them. The Minotaur had found his first victims.

"Damianos, I will miss you," Airlea's whispered, her courage wavering. She sank to the ground and waited, listening. Moments later, the Minotaur arrived. He circled Alex's daughter, sniffing at her. Then he looked at Alex, snorted, and scraped his back hooves across the ground, as he prepared to charge. As Alex backed away, the Minotaur tracked his movements.

"You can see me." Alex said. The Minotaur tossed his head and snorted louder. "Please spare my daughter," Alex pleaded. He could not stand by and watch her slaughtered.

"Minotaur! I am over here," Airlea yelled. "Why do you wait?"

With a great leap, the Minotaur landed inches away from

Airlea. He towered over her, grunting and pawing at the ground. Then he turned away. Alex breathed a sigh of relief. The Minotaur had spared her.

"Stop!" Airlea shouted. "You mistake me for a goddess. Hathor saved me, but my mother, Henhenet, was human. Five cycles I must complete before I am again powerful enough to fulfill my destiny. Help me move fully from Mount Olympus to Earth. Please, my courage is fading. Eat me. Eat me now!"

"No!" Alex screamed. He stood firmly between Airlea and the Minotaur. The Minotaur scuffed the ground and charged, passing straight through Alex. Airlea died in a few bloody seconds. The Minotaur departed without consuming her, leaving Alex to grieve. As Airlea's soul separated from her body, she looked, fondly, at Alex.

"It can't be," Alex whispered. Airlea's face changed to Anne's. "My sister was my daughter Airlea?" He had traced every aspect of his lives for clues, but never realized Anne's past lives intertwined with his. The missing parts the Bat wanted me to see, Alex realized, were the points when his and Anne's lives intersected.

Airlea's spirit morphed into an owl and took flight. She confidently navigated the complex passageways. Alex rushed after her through the Labyrinth. The gloom lifted where the end of the tunnel opened into a bright orange-and-pink sky. The owl settled atop a golden gate and gazed over the sea. Rays of morning sunlight flashed across the gate, splashing gold reflections into the tunnel. On the wall behind the gate, the reflections turned reddish-brown. Alex couldn't believe his eyes. Imbedded in the wall was the Carnelian Tablet. He traced his fingers over the symbols. He could read them! The moment he had long prepared for finally came. Behind him, the owl screeched and flew over the gate. The tablet symbols faded before Alex could memorize them. The Labyrinth was gone.

Alex now stood inside a prison cell where a young Asian woman, clasped in chains, wept. Anne had returned as a tortured slave. Her life was harsh, and she died young and alone. For hundreds of years, Alex watched in horror as Anne returned time and again as a slave — each new life more desperate than the last. He tried to help her, but in his ghostly form, he could do nothing. He wished with all his heart her next life would break this cycle, but she continued to be whipped, jailed, dragged in chains, and tortured. Every time she died, she prayed for salvation, only to return to an even worse existence. Alex fell into despair. This couldn't be what Airlea intended when she sacrificed her life to the Minotaur.

In her next life, Anne was not born into slavery. She was the only daughter of a farmer and his wife. Although she worked from dawn until late in the evening, at least she had some freedom. That began to change when nomads attacked their farm. Anne returned from tending the cattle to find their home ablaze and no sign of her parents. With nowhere else to turn, she brought the cattle to her only relative, her father's brother. It was in this man's home, considered a burden by him and a poor wretch by his wife, her enslavement started.

During the next six years, as they abused and neglected her, she began to resemble someone Alex knew. The day the cattle escaped, Alex was sure he had seen this life before and didn't want to see it again. Anne managed to round up the cattle, but not before one of them gored a woman in the village. When the woman's husband confronted Anne's uncle, demanding the bull be stoned to death, her uncle finally found his way to be rid of Anne. He claimed Anne had spirited the animal and that she was a witch. The man dragged her back to the village. Alex didn't follow. He knew this life — the life he pulled from Anne's soul during Grandmother's lesson. He couldn't bear to see the mob stone Anne to death again.

Anne returned as a Roman servant girl named Aelia. She had little freedom, but no one abused her. The lady of the house actually liked Aelia and treated her kindly. Alex didn't know the woman, but he recognized the seaside town, Herculaneum. He watched as the bond between Anne and the woman grew. The woman became ill, and her husband, a foul-tempered man, blamed Anne. The day his wife died, he chased Anne into the garden and beat her with a stick. Alex vividly recalled this day from his third life — the day Mount Vesuvius erupted.

Alex watched as the rest of his third and Anne's fourteenth life unfolded. Antonia, Alex in this life, ran into the garden. She yelled and pointed across the bay where the fires on Mount Vesuvius grew. Panic-stricken, the man ran away. Alex followed Antonia as she led the girl to her death in the sea.

"Finally, my pain will end. I am so tired," the girl lamented. She paused and stared at Alex's ghost. "First, I came from heaven back to earth. This time it must be by water in the midst of fire. You suffered through all my pain-filled lives. Thank you. Now a happier time will come."

Alex realized Anne had known he was with her. He remembered his — Antonia's — devastation as she watched the wave swallow the girl. Her remorse was intense, but Alex now realized this guilt was misplaced. As Airlea allowed the Minotaur to eat her to deliver her back to Earth, drowning under the tsunami would finally wash away Anne's suffering. When the sea calmed, monk seals played where she had died, delivering her into a new life.

Her sacrifice near Mount Vesuvius broke her cycle of torment. Anne spent her next seven lives creating magnificent art and healing people. She lived long, fulfilling lives until Alex and Anne's lives intersected again in 762 AD. Emperor Constantine V was leading a campaign to destroy all icons of Christ. Alex, a Christian priest in this life, opposed Constantine. The priest learned of an exceptional artist named Ariadne who lived on the outskirts of Constantinople. From her he commissioned a gold statue of Christ. Later that week, Constantine renewed his campaign to destroy icons. Anyone possessing forbidden items was tortured and killed. The priest hurried to warn Ariadne, but he was too late. Flames engulfed her house. Alex watched the priest scurry away to save himself.

This time, Alex swore, "I will not abandon Anne." He pushed through the flaming walls and found Ariadne beaten and barely conscious. The Emperor's soldiers had heaped gold and silver icons near her feet. The fire reached the roof and flaming beams fell around her. Thousands of spiders scrambled out of cracks in the floor.

"How wonderful!" Ariadne said, as she welcomed the spiders that covered her body, and bit into her flesh. "In the midst of metal, I die in fire." Later, Alex realized the spiders had paralyzed her to spare her the pain of burning alive.

Even though art and healing remained part of Anne's next

five lives, she concentrated on mastering science, philosophy, and theology. In the twelfth century, she was a nun named Guda who illuminated books about scriptures. Alex spotted his sister's mischievous grin as the nun drew her self-portrait in the initial letter of a "Homeliary." She laughed outright as she penned the inscription: "A sinner wrote and painted this book."

When Alex's fifth life collided with Anne's twenty-eighth, he knew what to expect. Alex was hunting in the woods and accidentally shot an old woman. For Alex, her dying words, "metal destroys me in the midst of my woods," had new meaning — Anne was moving into the next development cycle. Alex knew her next life would be better, but it pained him that her death, again, was his fault. A fox arrived to spirit her into her next life.

Alex chased the fox through a forest. At times he lost her, but the fox always backtracked to find him. When they reached a grassy field, the fox turned tail and disappeared. In the distance, Alex saw a massive medieval fortress. He followed a rutted dirt road to the drawbridge spanning the castle's moat. He walked across the bridge, under the portcullis, and through the main doors. In the castle's inner courtyard, a woman wearing an ornate dress watched a man plant a yew tree in a circular garden. Although she remained silent, Alex could tell the tree had deep meaning for her.

"Lady Anne," a gentlewoman said, "Your grandchildren are arriving."

"I will retire to the round room. Tell them I will greet them in the great hall within an hour," Lady Anne replied.

"My sister was a Lady?" Alex asked in surprise, but no one heard him and he saw no more of her in this life. Anne's lives now flashed by him like a movie on fast-forward. One minute Anne was mediating hostilities between an American Indian tribe and British colonists, and the next she was helping slaves through the Underground Railroad to Canada and freedom.

The fast-forward slowed as Alex's sixth life with Anne began. It was April 1908. Twenty-nine tornadoes hit thirteen states. One leveled their small town in Louisiana. Alex, Kate in this life, was Alice's best friend. When the tornado hit, Alice insisted they hide in her cellar. The tornado sucked up the house and collapsed the cellar, burying them alive. When Kate found Alice, she was already dead. A splintered beam had pierced her chest. Later that day, snakes slithered into the wreckage through a hole in the wall. Kate thanked God for the snakes. There was a way out, and she began digging around the hole.

"Killed by wood while buried under mounds of earth," Alex said, and he knew the snakes marked the beginning of the fifth and final cycle Anne had to endure.

Anne spent two lives trying to save the Earth's ecosystem before their lives crossed again. Anne, Avanti in this life, died in an earthquake in the Denali National Park in Alaska. Alex, her trail guide, ran away when a cougar appeared. The cat chased Avanti down a hillside to the lake. The earthquake split the lakebed, swallowing the water, Avanti and the cat through the crevasse.

As Avanti died, Alex's reality imploded, crashing him into his current life at the moment Anne was born. Alex had been born first and nearly died. Doctors whisked him to the neonatal intensive care ward. He knew from traversing his own life that two weeks would pass before he saw Anne again. Anne, born healthy, stayed with Mom and Aunt Selena who watched over Anne whenever Mom visited Alex. On the third day, while Aunt Selena helped Elizabeth prepare to leave the hospital, Marcus arrived. He gave Mom and Aunt Selena a kiss and then leaned over Anne's bassinette.

"Good morning, Mistress Anne. I have a gift for you," Marcus said, as he slipped a cloth scroll from a tube.

Alex's mom looked at the charcoal drawing. "It's a rubbing of Sir George's — your — armor. And you replaced Queen Elizabeth's cipher with two A's back to back," she said and kissed Marcus's cheek.

Alex looked at the charcoal rubbing recognizing the armor that attacked him at The Met.

Selena shook her head. "This will only complicate matters. You're not her father this time. Keep your past lives in the past."

Marcus ignored her. "Lady Anne, I have only had one life as a father. In that life, I wore this armor as Sir George Clifford, the Third Earl of Cumberland. Although I wasn't the best father back then, and I can never replace your dad, I promise in this life to be your champion."

Avanti's cougar, still wet with lake water, slunk into the room. Alex knew it was not here to guide Anne to her next life. It brushed past Marcus and pounced on Alex, taking him back in time, pausing every time Alex had killed Anne.

Alex awoke.

Morning fog drifted through the cave's triangular mouth. He was free of Anne's lives and had completed his vision quest. He now knew where to find the missing Carnelian Tablet symbols but, more importantly, he knew connecting the tablets was only his first task as the Amalgamator. In this life, Anne would confront the Plexians, as Enheduanna had centuries earlier. She was the Demagogue once more. He didn't know whose side the Bat was on, but knew opening a portal to the Plexus would unleash monsters. This time he vowed to stay by his sister's side. He also knew he had to be careful. If the pattern from their earlier lives continued, he would somehow cause her death.

"No! Not this time!" he yelled.

CHAPTER SIXTEEN

⊳𝕀𝕀𝕀⊲ ⊳𝕀𝕀𝕀⊲

THOTH'S SPELLS

Over night a cold front blew in, turning the air damp and chilly. Foggy wisps extended beyond the lake and coiled up the hill to a misty sky. Alex trudged through the woods toward the medical center. After his experience in the cave, he had new priorities: heal Anne, keep Anne from dying (in particular avoiding killing her himself), save Mom, stop Seth's experiments, and prevent the Plexians from entering his dimension. He had a clue how to approach only one of those goals. He knew Plexian poisons caused the burns on Anne's neck and had an idea how to heal her. The solution to the rest, he felt instinctively, revolved around finding the Primal Key. One problem at a time, he told himself.

As he reached the clearing near the medical center, he found George pacing on the road, talking to himself.

George saw Alex and ran to meet him. "Where have you been?"

"The cave on the far side of Ghost Lake."

"You actually went inside? Even Uncle Wayne won't go near that place. Aunt Selena is frantic. I'll let her know you're okay." George started to open his CyberNexus. Alex slapped it out of his hand.

"Hey! You'll break it!"

"No one can know I'm back — not yet," Alex said. "I need to get off the estate."

"Good luck with that. While you were gone, Lamia broke into Cleopatra's Needle. Bixia's worried she might access our transportation network. SANDY secured the entire estate. We're on lockdown. Isadora's moved anything even remotely connected with the tablets to the artifact room — even the family portraits. Aunt Margaret is furious about the forced relocation. She actually called Isadora a paranoid autocrat."

"Did Isadora move Anne, too?" Alex asked, wondering exactly what constituted being "connected to the tablets." After his trip through Anne's lives he knew she had mastered all of them in her past. She was the glue that would connect them and reveal the location of the Primal Key. At least he hoped she could. If she really was the next Demagogue, she needed to return the Key or the Plexian demon (a.k.a. the Bat) would cause the Earth's demise.

"Anne's still in the medical center. I checked in on her this morning. She's conscious and cranky. Those red burns on her neck are worse. She says it feels like bees are trying to sting their way out from under her skin. Helena thinks it's energy spider venom. Bakari hasn't left her side since yesterday." George suppressed a smirk.

"It's not the spiders. A Plexian jellyfish stung her. Somehow, when Anne became Enheduanna, the jellyfish stings imprinted on her, too." Alex could tell George wasn't following his logic. Alex sighed. "I'll explain later. Right now I need to get to The Met."

George laughed at the idea. "There's no way SANDY will let you leave. I'm surprised she hasn't detected you already."

Alex let desperation flood into his voice, knowing George would hear and feel his anxiety. "That's why I need your help. You've lived here all your life. There must be a way off the estate. If I don't get the cure, Anne could die. Enheduanna lasted fourteen hours after the attack. I don't know how much longer Anne can hang on."

George rubbed his chin. "Well, there is a way, but it's risky. I can't manage the transportation logistics, but Chasca can. I'm not sure she'll risk another suspension, though." George hurried Alex back into the woods. "If this is going to work, we'll have to stay off SANDY's radar. Avoid the main paths and buildings."

"I need a healer and an alchemist, too." Alex said.

"Olivia will jump at the chance, but I'm not sure I can get a healer to break the rules. Helena isn't a forgiving master."

"What about Bakari?"

"He's chosen an assassin's path. Healing is not in his DNA,

but he did stay with Anne all night. I'll try to convince him. Meet us in the woods across from the orchard."

To avoid SANDY, Alex picked his way around the wild roses, blackberry thickets and prickly barberry bushes that cluttered the woods. When he reached the orchard, Chasca was waiting impatiently for him. She gave him a big hug then looked at him sternly. "You're going to get me suspended again — or worse."

Before Alex could respond, Olivia, George and Bakari pushed through the bushes. "Sorry it took us so long," George said, handing Alex a bottle of water and pizza wrapped in a wad of paper towels. "I figured you missed breakfast, so I grabbed some leftovers from the fridge."

"Isadora is going to flip when she finds out you're back," Bakari said. "Anyone who's not preparing to raid Seth's bases is looking for you."

Olivia rolled her eyes. "So they can look a little longer." She turned to Alex. "So, what's the scam and how can we help?"

Alex inhaled the crushed slices of cold pepperoni pizza then chugged the water before explaining. "I went on a vision quest last night."

"Did Cosmo the Frog's wax help?" Bakari asked.

"Didn't need it." Alex reached into his pocket to retrieve the vial of frog goo.

"Keep it," Bakari insisted. "You never know when you might need to puke your way through a vision."

"During my quest, I saw the missing Carnelian Tablet symbols."

"You did it!" Chasca cheered. "I knew you would find the tablet."

"I saw them when I was in one of Anne's past lives, but the symbols faded before I could read them. So, first we cure Anne and when she's strong enough she can help me see the tablet again."

"What type of cure?" Bakari asked, skeptically. "Even Helena's stumped."

"Water from the Magical Stela," Alex said, stuffing the pizza-stained towel and empty bottle into his jacket pocket. "We need to get to The Met, find Priestess Henhenet and convince her to make the anti-venom."

George threw his hands in the air. "That's your plan! Are you crazy? You can't face Henhenet! What if she tries to possess you?"

Alex grinned. "I'm counting on it. Now, how do we get off the estate?"

"George's shack," Chasca answered. "It's the only portal off Isadora's transportation grid." She smiled at George's surprised expression. "Your dad told me where to find it. I guess he sensed I needed a break once in a while."

George turned pale. "You've been inside my place!"

"Of course not. That thing's about to collapse," Chasca said with disgust. "I can access the portal from outside, but with a group this size, we'll have to go inside your shack."

George's complexion raced through pinks and reds, settling into a purple-blue tint. He's going to nix the plan, Alex thought. Instead George blew out a long, unsteady breath. "This had better work."

Without another word, George led them across the road into the vineyard. He timed their move between the rows of grape vines to avoid SANDY's cameras. At the vineyard's edge, a gravel road stretched away from the swamp toward the farmhouse. George pointed in the opposite direction toward the misty swamp. "We'll have to get past those trees to Trout Creek. It's beyond SANDY's reach. When I say go, run as fast as you can."

George stared at the irrigation system moving through the field. Although Alex couldn't see SANDY's camera, he guessed it was somewhere on the series of pipes. "GO!" George said and sprinted up the gravel road into the mounds of swamp grass. When they reached the safety of the trees, they paused to catch their breath.

"We should be far enough in now," George said. "SANDY can't detect us in here. We'll stay close to Trout Creek until it joins Shades of Death River — just to be safe."

Alex heard a distant dog howl; several other dogs responded.

"Great!" George said. "SANDY must have seen us. She released the hounds."

"SANDY's siccing dogs on us?" Olivia laughed to mask her fear.

"They sound pretty far away," Chasca said hopefully.

"Can't you use your Agate talents? Talk to them. Convince them to leave us alone," Bakari suggested, fading in and out of sight as his camo-instincts took over.

"When I'm by myself they listen — sometimes. But the pack loves a chase. Make sure you stay near the creek. They hate the mud. It sticks to everything."

The dogs reached the other side of the creek, growling and bearing their teeth as their paws raked the ground.

"We have to get to the river before them," George said, and took off at a full run.

As he ran, Alex risked taking his eyes off the rutted path to check on the pack. The dogs remained on the other side of the creek, but kept pace. "George they're gaining on us. What happens if they reach the river before us?"

"There's a ruined bridge across the creek near the river. It's a long jump, but the larger dogs can get across. If they make it, our only choice is to wade into the river and call my dad for help."

They reached the bridge across Trout Creek, out of breath, but they couldn't rest, the pack was nearing. Up ahead, Alex could hear Shades of Death River. It sounded big, fast, and angry. The dogs reached the bridge as George led the way down the steep riverbank. Chasca stumbled, belly-flopping in the mud. Alex stooped to help her up, but froze. Across the river, five ghosts laid on the muddy bank. Worse, a dozen or more men and women floated under the water, their mouths gaping and their eyes vacant.

George yelled, "The dogs are almost here." He pulled a canoe from behind a bush to the river's edge. Grabbing a coil of rope from the hull, he quickly looped the rope around a tree root jutting out of the riverbank. "Grab the paddles and get in."

Alex jolted from his stupor and helped Chasca into the boat.

George tied the other end of the rope to a handle on the boat. "I'll keep the rope from tangling. Paddle hard and fast or we won't reach the other side."

George eased out the rope and the current swept the boat downstream. "Alex! Bakari! Paddle!" he yelled.

Alex looked at George and then at the faces in the river. He couldn't bear to push the oar through their heads.

"I've got this," Olivia said taking the paddle from him.

"George, when I say now, let the rope slack," Olivia said calmly.

"If I let go too soon we will land on THIS side of the river," George croaked, looking at the three dogs bounding along the top of the riverbank.

"Trust me," Olivia insisted.

The dogs raced down to the river's edge, bearing their teeth and kicking up mud.

"Now!" Olivia yelled.

George loosened his grip on the rope and the canoe shot downstream, but Olivia managed to time each stroke perfectly and, with minimal effort on her part, they made it across the river.

"Nicely navigated," Bakari said.

Olivia shrugged. "When I was ten, I aced my first Alchemy test: finding beauty and structure in chaos. River currents are easy."

A chill ran up Alex's leg as he realized Olivia had landed the raft on one of the sleeping ghosts. The ghost stirred and sat up, his torso sticking up through the canoe.

The ghost shouted thrusting his fist toward the sky. "Oh, please God, no! How long must I pay?" He waded, ankle deep, into the river, sank down and wept.

The dog's barks became frenzied, as the ghost's weeping turn to deep sobs.

"Uncle Wayne told me he released all the ghosts roaming the

estate," Alex said, jumping out of the boat.

"There are ghosts — here?" George asked, glancing around nervously.

"Five men on the shore and about a dozen people in the river. By the way they're dressed, it looks like they've been here more than a century."

"You can see me?" The ghost asked Alex, astonished.

"I'm Alex. What is your name?" Uncle Wayne had taught Alex to start with names. Sometimes ghosts didn't know they were dead, and telling them was not a polite way to start a conversation. After the formalities, he needed to keep the ghost talking to understand what trapped him here and determine if he was dangerous.

"My name?" The ghost struggled to remember. "Edward . . . Edward Devillin."

"How did you end up in this swamp?" Alex asked.

"Malaria infected all of us. My wife, Sarah, and our children were the sickest. I thought cutting through the swamp would save a day's travel to the doctor in Hope Village. Alas, the storm came. It rained for five days, flooding the river. The waters destroyed the bridges and the swamp became unpassable. By the time the ground began to dry, we were all too sick to travel. It is my fault we died here!"

A horrible thought crossed Alex's mind. "Were the people in the water part of your group?"

"Yes." A translucent tear trickled down his cheek. "There are moments in between malaria attacks when your mind is your own again. During one such break, my wife begged me to kill

166

her. That night, we agreed that when the malaria returned, I would throw her in the river. Drowning seemed the most compassionate way to end her life. Others begged for the same release, and the five of us still strong enough granted their wishes. Three days later, the illness took us as well. For our sins, God punishes us. My wife's soul is trapped in the river and I am doomed to relive the pain of malaria for eternity."

"Alex, what's going on?" George asked. He and the others couldn't hear the ghost, but could tell by Alex's questions that something horrible had happened here. Alex quickly explained.

"They murdered everybody!" Bakari exclaimed, fading into the pattern of the tree bark behind him.

"The pain! He has no idea!" Edward wailed. For a moment, the barking dogs fell silent. "The attack is sudden and brutal. Sunlight burns a hole in your head and even the voices of your loved ones are like shards of glass piercing your brain. The chills are unbearable. You tremble uncontrollably as pain permeates your entire body. You beg for help and then you wish for death. But when Archangel Michael and even dreaded Samael pass you by, you collapse like a rag doll, no substance or form left in your muscles."

"Where are your children?" Alex asked. "I only see adults."

"Our children's souls are safe. They died before the storm ended. I buried them on a high point near the bridge."

Alex wanted to help release this man's soul, but that would take time — time Anne didn't have to spare. The three dogs on the other side of the river howled and ran toward Trout Creek. The rest of the pack began barking. They were on the move again.

"Alex we need to leave — now," George said. "The pack knows where I'm headed. Now that we crossed the river, they will take another path to Bear Island."

Alex turned back to the ghost. "I can help you break your cycle of pain, but I have to take care of my sister first. I promise I'll return."

Edward dropped to his knees. "Thank you, and thank the Lord. Having a ray of hope lifts my spirits."

A ghost further down the riverbank stirred and sat up. Edward hurried to his side and helped him stand. They spoke briefly and the ghost floated up river.

Edward returned to Alex. "Joseph agreed to help. We cannot leave the swamp, but we can guard the bridges. The dogs will not cross the river while we bar their way. We will keep them at bay as long as possible, but our malaria attacks will soon come."

Before Alex could thank him, Edward flew up river to defend the bridge. The pack barked and growled at the ghosts.

"We'd better hurry," George said, running along a ridge that cut above the swamp water. "My boardwalk is beyond those willow trees."

Although George's boardwalk wasn't New Jersey shore quality, the slippery plywood sheets connecting the grass mounds were solid. After ten minutes of careful navigation (although Olivia frequently bounded ahead and circled back like she was playing a simple game of hopscotch around the others), they arrived on Bear Island. The island, a crescent shaped, half-mile long mound rose out of the swamp like a deflating beach ball. On the island's highest point sat George's shack. He hurried to the shack and stood with his back to the front door, blocking their way.

"What's wrong?" Olivia asked.

"You must promise not to make fun of my place," George said, "not even one chuckle."

Chasca flicked more mud off her shirt and shook her wet shoes. "Believe me. I'm not in a laughing mood." She pushed past him.

Inside, life-sized posters of Batman and Spiderman stared at each other from opposing walls. Alex didn't recognize the third superhero, who wore a dark blue mask, form-fitting green tights, and a long-sleeved shirt. On his chest, inside a sky blue oval rimmed with gold, was a bright green symbol.

"The Agate Avenger?" Chasca asked, reading the title of the poster. "Is that supposed to be you?"

"Look, he even has Anne's funny toothbrush-key on his chest," Olivia said. She saw a stack of drawings on the table and began leafing through them. "The Adventures of the Agate Avenger — flexible as bamboo and as solid as a mighty oak," she read. "Did you write these comic strips?"

George flopped into a beat-up lawn chair in the corner of the room. "Why did I let you in here? What was I thinking?" His embarrassment flooded the room.

"I love it!" Olivia said, continuing to peruse the comics. "It's perfect! You've covered every Agate Tablet talent, although I didn't know Agate Tablet masters could fly," she teased.

George blushed, his mood lightened until Chasca grabbed a book from his desk. "You shouldn't have an Advanced Agate Textbook. You just passed your first trial," she said, tapping her finger on the book's cover.

"It's my dad's," George admitted. "I've been practicing for

years. I can do most of the Agate Tablet stuff." George smiled mischievously. "I even started a batch of energy matter."

"Outside the lab!" Chasca exclaimed, frantically looking around the room. "That stuff can explode."

"It's completely contained," George insisted. "It's almost done. Want to see? It's beautiful."

"Absolutely," Bakari said.

Alex grabbed George's arm. "We don't have time for the V.I.P. tour. Where's the portal?"

George pointed at the Agate Avenger.

"You're sure you can take all of us?" Bakari asked.

Chasca rolled her eyes. "I've got this covered. Hold hands and don't let go." Chasca pulled them through the superhero and into the Temple of Dendur in The Met.

"Hey, you! The museum's closed," a security guard said, giving them a dirty look.

"Sorry. We didn't know," Alex said, hurrying down the steps and along the reflecting pool.

As he reached the gallery exit, Emma intercepted him. "What do you think you are doing?" she demanded. "Isadora is beside herself. You must return to —"

"I think Henhenet can cure Anne," Alex interrupted her.

Emma regarded him thoughtfully. "The Stela?"

Alex nodded. "Anne's been poisoned by a Plexian jellyfish."

Emma spoke with a security guard. He looked shocked, glared at the kids and then spoke into his comm-pad.

"Directive from the Director: Seal off the Egyptian Art Galleries," a pleasant voice said from speakers throughout the museum.

"You have one hour," Emma told Alex. "The museum must open on schedule." Emma frowned as she looked at Chasca's muddy shirt and shoes and the footprints across the gallery floor. "You, young lady, will stay here. The maintenance crews have enough to do without cleaning up after you."

"I'm not staying here while Alex faces Henhenet," Chasca snapped. She slipped off her sneakers and marched in muddy socks toward Gallery 128.

"Is Henhenet here?" Bakari asked nervously.

Alex scanned the room overflowing with ghosts, but Henhenet was nowhere in sight. "I hope she's not in Cairo," he said, skirting the edge of the room.

"We keep her sarcophagus in another gallery. Perhaps she is there," Emma suggested. Alex cringed as he watched Emma walk through the ghosts.

Henhenet's empty sarcophagus occupied one corner of Gallery 104. "She's not here either," Alex said, his frustration growing.

"Who's this guy?" George asked, studying a large stone statue in the center of the room.

"King Mentuhotep II. Henhenet was one of his lower-ranking wives," Emma explained.

"Lower-ranking?" Chasca asked with distain. "How many wives did this jerk have?"

"Seven we know of," Emma replied. "Wayne tried to speak with Henhenet about life in the eleventh dynasty. She got a little upset. The results were not pretty. It's a pity! We could learn so much from her."

All I need from Henhenet is Anne's cure, Alex thought. He

wandered into a darker gallery past little models of Egyptian boats. The sign on the wall claimed the objects in the room were from Mentuhotep's Deir el-Bahari temple. As he rounded the corner, he found the priestess asleep near a small sarcophagus. Alex rapped his knuckles against the glass. Her eyes flew open, and she glared at Alex with contempt.

"You," she hissed. "Leave me in peace. I do not wish to speak with the living."

"But I need your help," Alex pleaded.

"No!" Henhenet exclaimed.

"It's about your daughter," Alex pressed.

"I have no daughter!" she insisted.

"But the goddess, Hathor —"

"Do not speak her name! The goddess of motherhood — I would spit on her! Where was she when I needed her! I died giving birth to the Pharaoh's child. My child died as well."

"Hathor saved your daughter. The moment before she died, the goddess brought her into herself," Alex said.

"You try to trick me —"

"No, honestly. My sister, Anne, was your daughter. I went into her past life and watched you die. Anne's really sick. She's been poisoned."

"My daughter's heart would be as light as Ma'at's feather. She should be in the fields of reeds . . . . How can my daughter live again? Why would the gods send her soul back?"

"Because Anne must face monsters stronger than your gods," Alex replied.

The priestess jumped out of the display case into Alex's body. "If you lie, I will haunt you for eternity," Alex heard her say in his mind. Then his mind blanked as Henhenet possessed him.

Alex pointed at Emma. "You! Bring me the Life of Spirit dish," Henhenet demanded in Alex's voice.

"Alex, watch your tone —" Emma scolded.

"I don't think that's Alex," Chasca said.

"Definitely not," George agreed. "Who are you?" he asked tentatively.

"I am Henhenet and a priestess of Hathor once more. Bring me the dish."

Emma opened her mouth to say something. Only "huh" made it out.

"You do not know your own collection? Do you leave everything to your curators?" Henhenet let out an irritated snort. "The dish of Ka and Ankh. You call it a 'libation dish.' It is in Gallery 101."

Emma said nothing, nodded and hurried out of the gallery.

Henhenet turned to Bakari. "Healer, come with me. To save my daughter you must become Horus. I will be Isis. She," Henhenet said, pointing at Olivia, "must be Thoth."

"What about us?" George asked, standing next to Chasca.

"Watch in silence," Henhenet said, dismissing him.

Emma joined them in Gallery 128, cradling the stone libation dish in her arms.

"Give the dish to Thoth," Henhenet instructed.

"That would be me," Olivia said. Emma gasped as Olivia pried the priceless dish away from her.

"Open this case," Henhenet demanded, pointing to the Plexiglas surrounding the Stela.

"But —" Emma began to object.

"I command you!" Henhenet bellowed.

Emma held her breath as she unlocked and lifted the display case off the Stela.

"Now bring me one other item, the Bes Amulet in Gallery 127. Make sure you bring the blue-green ceramic Bes. My daughter will need all the protection she can get when she faces these monsters."

As Emma scurried to find the amulet, Henhenet pulled a laminated card out of a box attached to the display case. "As you cannot speak my language, we will improvise using James Allen's translation of the story and Nora Scott's spells . . . . I do miss Nora."

One of the ghosts in the gallery inched closer to look at the card.

"Back!" Henhenet ordered. "All of you away." The ghosts scattered into the adjacent galleries.

Henhenet tapped her lips with her fingertips. "Now, which water to use? New York's finest? Fresh rainwater would be best," she decided.

"I can make it rain," George offered.

"Yeah, right," Chasca scoffed. "Controlling the weather is Level Five. Simon just passed it yesterday."

"Fine, I'll prove it. One rainy day at The Met coming up," George said.

"Are you sure about this?" Chasca asked. "Simon's storm had lightning —"

"Trust me I know what I'm doing," George said. He closed his eyes to concentrate. A breeze blew through the gallery and a gentle rain fell from the ceiling.

"You did it," Olivia said in amazement.

"Place the dish at the Stela's base," Henhenet said, as the rainwater began to trickle down. "Remember your parts."

"Anne has been stung! Anne has been stung! Thoth, great is your heart! Have you come equipped with magic and bearing the great command of justice, one remedy after another, without number? See, Anne suffers with poison." Henhenet pointed to a line on the laminated card.

Olivia read, "Don't fear! Don't fear, divine Isis! Anne, Anne, let your heart be resolute and not weaken because of the poison's fire!"

"Now," Henhenet said to Bakari.

Bakari read the spell. "Flow out, poison, approach, come forth on earth. Turn, beast, take away your poison, which is in Anne's body. Behold, the magic of Horus is too strong for you. Flow out, poison!"

Henhenet nodded in satisfaction. "That should work."

"What have you done?" Emma yelled, splashing water as she stomped into the room.

"I guess my muddy shoes don't seem so bad now," Chasca snickered.

Henhenet glared at Emma and snatched the amulet from her. She gave it and the libation dish to Bakari. "Sprinkle this water on my daughter's wounds. After the poison leaves her body, she must drink the remaining liquid in the dish." Henhent reached into Alex's jacket and retrieved the water bottle. She chanted in Egyptian as she filled it with Stela-infused water.

After returning the bottle to Alex's pocket, Henhenet stepped out of his body. Control of his mind returned. He shuddered and wiped his hands across his arms, pushing away the remnants of Henhenet's energy. His voice quivered as he thanked the priestess.

She nodded politely and said, "After Anne slays the monsters, ask my daughter to visit me."

CHAPTER SEVENTEEN

SURVIVING THE SURGE

They left Emma to deal with the flooded gallery and returned to the estate. Isadora, who was furious, intercepted them in the transportation center. "SANDY! Reset the transportation grid — lock it down! And revoke Chasca's transportation privileges while you're at it." Isadora, her face almost the color of the Carnelian tablet, turned on Chasca. "What were you thinking? We can only hope Seth wasn't monitoring The Met."

"It's not her fault," Alex said. "I asked them to —"

"Yes, I know, help concoct a miracle cure," Isadora waved away the idea. "I understand you created quite a mess."

"Henhenet used the Stela. We have to try it," Bakari said, carefully raising the libation dish for Isadora to inspect.

Isadora sniffed the ozone laced water. "Rubbish, why would Henhenet help you?"

"I let her possess me," Alex answered.

Isadora's eyes widened, softening her scowl.

As Alex recounted their trip to The Met and his night in the cave, Isadora's anger dissolved. By the time he got to the part about seeing the Carnelian tablet in Anne's past life, her eyes gleamed with excitement. She smoothed her shirt with her hands and squared her shoulders. "Bakari and Alex come with me."

The kids followed Isadora out of the transportation center into the Crystal hallway. "Not everyone," Isadora said. Anne doesn't need you crowding into her recovery room. Chasca, go help Abigail. She's coordinating transportation logistics. The strike team leaves tomorrow. They'll attack Seth's compound at dusk." She turned to Olivia. "Go to the command center. I'm sure there is plenty of chaos there to keep you busy."

"What about me?" George asked, avoiding Isadora's eyes.

"Your dad is putting the final touches on the insect attack plans. I'm sure he could use your help."

George brightened. "Really? You want me to help Dad?"

Isadora shooed him away. "Go, before I change my mind."

Alex and Bakari followed Isadora to the medical center, remaining silent, hoping Isadora's excitement about the Carnelian Tablet would keep her anger at bay.

Helena met them outside Anne's room. "Anne's conscious, but disoriented. I asked Simon to monitor her emotions and . . . umm . . . fluctuating personalities." Helena looked distastefully at Bakari's libation dish. "You're certain the Priestess's motives were — altruistic?"

"No," Alex replied. "Her reasons for helping are selfish, but her intentions are good. She longs to see her daughter."

"Let's hope it doesn't kill her." Helena reached for the bowl.

Bakari pulled it to his body protectively. "I need to administer it to Anne."

"Has my little assassin finally turned to healing?" Helena asked, skeptically.

Bakari smirked and carefully carried the bowl into Anne's room, where Simon sat next to Anne's bed, holding her hand.

"She's barely conscious now," Simon told Helena without taking his gaze from Anne's face. "Lately, I sense more Priestess than Anne. She believes she's dying inside an ancient temple." He turned toward Alex. "I'm sorry, I'm sure that sounds crazy."

"Not at all. Anne's past is — complicated." Alex nodded to Bakari.

Simon wrinkled his nose at the water in the dish. "What is that stuff? It smells like welding fumes."

Bakari ignored Simon. "If this works, I swear I'll switch to healing," he promised. Acting as Horus, he recited the spell. "Flow out, poison, approach, come forth on earth. Turn, beast, take away your poison, which is in Anne's body. Behold, the magic of Horus is too strong for you. Flow out, poison!"

Anne trembled as Bakari sprinkled the serum along her neck. The blisters oozed yellowy-pink liquid as the serum bubbled and hissed.

Simon dropped her hand and leaned back in his chair. "Their minds — they melded."

Alex hadn't anticipated this side-effect. Was Anne still — Anne? He leaned over her bed. "Anne?" he asked, tentatively.

As her blisters began to shrink, her eyes flickered open. Anne licked her chapped lips. "You're such a jerk," she rasped. "Where have you been?"

Alex grinned — definitely still Anne. "I spent last night in a cave —" Alex began.

Anne laughed weakly. "Oh, right, Mr. Claustrophobic went inside a cave. Like I'm going to believe —"

"Honestly! I went on a . . . well, I don't know where I went, but I traveled through your past lives — all thirty-six of them."

"You trespassed on my lives!" Anne exclaimed, pushing herself up on her elbows. "Alex, you promised not to — not ever!"

"I didn't have a choice! Let me finish," Alex said. "You really were Princess Enheduanna, and I watched you — I mean her — create the dodecahedron. When she opened it, Plexian jellyfish attacked her. She stopped them, but her injuries were too great. She died, but that turned out okay, because you came back as Henhenet's daughter. When Henhenet died in childbirth, Hathor saved you. Henhenet's the one who helped cast the spell on the healing water. By the way, I promised her you would visit her."

"Alex, stop," Anne said, sinking back onto the pillows. "You're giving me a headache." She rubbed her temples with her fingers.

"We should let her rest," Helena decided. "Simon, go check in with Thomas. He wants to finalize the strike team plans today."

"The attack? It's today?" Anne asked.

"Tomorrow," Simon replied.

"Did Marcus find Mom? Did the clue from my dream-painting help?"

Simon took Anne's hand in his. "No one knows what 'ect Greek Island' means. Seth doesn't own property in Greece. It's a dead end."

"It must mean something," Anne insisted. "Alex, my painting should be dry. Find Chasca. She can take you inside it to look for more clues."

"If Henhenet is right, in a few more minutes, you can lead the search yourself," Bakari said, cheerfully.

"Who's Henhenet again?" Anne asked, now sitting on the edge of the bed.

"Your mother — life number two," Alex replied.

Simon helped Anne stand.

"Well, now that Anne's on the mend, I have my own preparations to attend to," Isadora said.

"For your trip to Nazca?" Anne asked, holding onto Simon to steady herself.

Isadora glared at Anne.

"Your self-portrait told me. She also said you never planned to give Seth the Key."

"That woman's half-crazy, but correct. The dodecahedron will remain locked in the artifact room. I plan to uncover whatever mischief Seth's agents are causing in Nazca and Marcus will —"

"Mom's not in Texas," Anne insisted. "What if Marcus can't stop Seth's experiment? Mom will —"

"We'll all — the entire world will be altered," Isadora finished.

"But your self-portrait needs Mom to heal her. The painting's not — normal. She's already convinced Lady Brunel to destroy part of her world."

"Lady Brunel is nearing retirement," Isadora said, sadly. "Even Elizabeth's best pigments can't stop her decline. My painted self is helping her slowly shut down her world.

"That's cruel!" Bakari exclaimed.

"Better than turpentine," Isadora hissed. "Do you have a better solution?" Alex could see rage building in her eyes.

Helena stepped in front of Bakari, shielding him. Isadora pasted on a tight smile. "Simon," Isadora said, still glaring at Helena, "Get back to insect preparations. Helena, why don't you accompany me to the Tablet Complex? I would like you to set up the battle triage center in the Onyx Tablet hall on the transportation level."

Simon squeezed Anne's hand, "I'll be back as soon as I can," he promised.

As Isadora reached the door, she turned and stared at Alex. "If Anne is the Demagogue, as you claim, she will need more than Bruegel's sphere this time. Contact me immediately after you retrieve the missing section of the tablet."

"Do you really know where to find the tablet?" Anne asked. "And what did she call me — a demon-god?"

"A demagogue. Enheduanna was the last one. It's your turn in this life." Alex paused, waiting to see how Anne took the news. She sat on the bed looking more confused than upset. Alex pressed on. "When I watched your third life, I saw the Carnelian Tablet — the whole tablet. On the bottom there is a Plexian death and rebirth spell." Alex shook his head and let out an uneasy chuckle. "Before I could finish examining it, you landed us in prison."

"Prison?" Anne said in disbelief.

"Never mind that part. If we could stop at the right moment in time, I'm sure I could read the tablet and find the real Key."

"But the dodecahedron —" Anne protested.

"Connects the tablets, but it's not the Key. The Bat took me on the vision quest so I could see when our past lives crossed and see the missing symbols. The Bat told me, 'the Primal Key must wake before the Earth's great quake.' I'm sure he meant Seth's experiment."

"Even if you find the Key, Isadora won't give it to Seth," Bakari pointed out. "Ever since Anne found the dodecahedron, Isadora's been maniacal about protecting the Collective's secrets."

"I'm not going to give the Key to Seth, either. Anne needs it to stop the Plexians."

"We'll save Mom first, then we'll figure out how to stop the Plexians," Anne decided.

"I don't think they can be separated. Your Plexian monster told Enheduanna the next demagogue must return the Key or cause Earth's demise. Mom — all of us — die if we don't give back the Key in time."

Anne crinkled her brow. "So, how do we wake up a key?"

Alex shrugged, "We'll figure that out when we find it."

Anne looked away, staring out the window. "Alex, there's something I need to tell you. In my dream, the energy spiders told me, 'The Curse is upon us. Stop the Amalgamator. Awaken the Key.' Alex, maybe you're the one who needs to stop before you cause death and destruction. Maybe you should —"

"No!" Alex insisted, although the same thought had been

rattling around in his mind. "There must be another Amalgamator."

"Seth?" Bakari suggested. "You said he has Bruegel's spheres. He's using them for his experiments."

"Maybe, but then why are his experiments failing?"

"Dad thought Bruegel was an Amalgamator, Alchemist and a Transcender. Even then he only managed to open a breach." Anne said. "Maybe you need the whole package. All the tablet talents . . . ." She trailed away in thought.

Alex placed his hand on Anne's shoulder. "Let's find the missing tablet symbols and the Key. We'll figure this out, together. I promise to keep you safe."

"So we just go into my past and get the tablet. It sounds too easy," Anne said. "You're not telling me something."

Alex tried to think of a way to break the news to Anne gently, but there was no way to sugarcoat her death. "I saw the tablet when we left the Labyrinth, after the Minotaur attacked you."

"If Anne got Enheduanna's burns when she channeled her, what will a Minotaur attack do," Bakari asked, protectively.

Anne studied Bakari and then Alex. She let out a deep breath. "Okay. We'll go, but make it fast. I hate this myth."

Alex smiled. "I guess now you know why."

"When we go into my past life, will I feel anything?"

Alex thought about the Minotaur's swift kill. "I don't think it will hurt too much. It will seem real, but when we come back, you should be yourself again."

Alex sat on the edge of her bed and put out his hands. As Anne touched them, she was born in Athens as Airlea. Together, they traversed her life.

✠✠✠✠

Alex had seen Airlea's courage in the Labyrinth and now marveled at the kindness she showed the other children on their voyage to Crete. She cared for them when they were seasick, sang the youngest girls to sleep and led their daily prayers. Once they arrived, she refused to attend King Minos's feast and cursed him for his vengeful acts. The next morning Minos and his soldiers led the children to the Labyrinth's gate.

Airlea pleaded with Minos, "Must you kill fourteen children? Let my one life be retribution for your son's death. Let the others go."

"It is not nearly enough!" Minos snarled. His soldiers pushed the children into the Labyrinth and locked the gate.

Alex followed Airlea as she skipped through the passageways. He watched in disgust as the Minotaur took her life — again. He waited by her body for the spirit owl to rise. Nothing happened. He tried to remember the direction the owl flew during his vision quest. Should I try going alone? He wondered. No, he knew he would get lost in the Labyrinth and lose his link to Anne. With no other safe options, Alex returned with Anne to their current life.

✠✠✠✠

Anne opened her eyes in horror and clutched her throat. Beads of blood dotted a scratch where the Minotaur had struck. "I am not doing that again!"

"Finish the water," Bakari said, handing Anne the libation dish. "Henhenet insisted you drink all of it."

Anne drank without hesitation and the scratch scabbed over.

"Tell me you got what you needed."

"It didn't work. Once you died, nothing else happened," Alex said. "What do you remember?"

Anne's eyes widened as past memories surfaced. "Only bits. Airlea had a lot of the goddess Hathor in her. That's why Airlea knew she must face the Minotaur to start the five cycles of change. A creature of the gods needed to kill her so she could return, fully, in an earthly form."

Alex told her, "In the cave, animal spirits led me through your lives. It started with the Bat. He created a shatter point and dropped me into Enheduanna's life. I was stuck there until an army of frogs escorted me into Airlea's life."

"I remember the frogs covering Enheduanna's dead body. They carried her spirit, cleansing and transforming her into Henhenet's daughter." Anne shuddered. "Alex, I don't like this past life stuff. It's too weird."

"Do you remember the owl? Was it real, too?" Alex asked.

"It had mottled wings and a large round head. It released me from the Labyrinth," Anne replied.

"I think I should tell you about your other lives. In life number three you were a slave." He walked Anne through her eleven lives in bondage, sparing her the most brutal moments. "You ended your first transformational phase after a tsunami killed you." Alex paused and took a deep breath. "I was part of that life. I led you to the water."

"You let me drown!" Anne exclaimed.

"I didn't know you were planning to kill yourself! Besides, you seemed to know it was time. Your seal guides took you to a happy, inspired place. Your next seven lives were great.

You were a healer and an artist. That is, until I left you in your burning house."

Bakari shook his head and laughed nervously. "Let me guess. Every time your lives cross, you do something to kill Anne."

Alex looked at the ground. He couldn't bring himself to admit it.

"You do? You kill me every time?" Anne asked, shocked.

"Only when you're in a transformational life," Alex said, defensively. "And I don't always kill you. Sometimes I just stand by and watch you die." That sounded even worse, he realized, feeling guilt crash inside his heart.

"How often did our lives cross?" Anne asked.

"Eight times, including our current life; but, Anne, I promise to keep you safe this time. I promise."

Anne frowned. "Tell me about the rest of my lives."

Alex recounted her next twenty-one lives, spending extra time on the transformational ones. When he admitted he left her in Alaska to die when an earthquake swallowed her and an entire lake, she looked like she might puke.

"Each of your transformational lives was linked to a tablet, and you're developing cross-tablet talents. Somehow, you unite them." Anne didn't fight the idea, but Alex thought she didn't fully accept it. He felt a prickling on his neck as Anne studied him.

"When I was Enheduanna, you watched me create the dodecahedron, and for the few seconds when I focused on each symbol, you could read it before it turned into gibberish, just like the tablet in Lady Brunel's painting. Maybe, at a different point in Dumont's memory —"

"I've been thinking about that. Do you remember seeing Dumont carrying a rolled up cloth on his way out of the hold?" Alex asked.

"I don't remember much, except the waves rocking the ship," Anne said, her face turning pale from the memory.

"Trust me; he did. If the cloth was protecting the tablet, why would he remove it? When I was in the cave, I also saw parts of our current life. When you were a baby, Marcus gave you a charcoal rubbing of a piece of armor. It was on cloth, too."

Anne scrunched her face in disgust. "Why did he do that?"

"I don't know," Alex lied, deciding Anne wouldn't want to hear about her past life with Marcus. "What if Dumont took a rubbing of the tablet like the one Marcus gave you."

"But wouldn't the rubbings be blurry just like the tablet?" Bakari asked.

"I don't think so. Lady Brunel told us his subconscious thoughts made it into the paintings. Maybe, at the very moment he rubbed the tablet, the symbols imprinted in his mind," Alex said.

Anne's expressions softened. "There's only one way to find out, but you owe me big for this one. I hate getting seasick."

"This is all very interesting," Bakari interrupted, "but Anne's in no condition to go inside Lady Brunel's dying painting or aboard the *Chevrette*."

Anne brushed her hand across her neck, gently probing where the jellyfish had stung her. "No, if I really am the Demagogue, I'll need the spheres and the Key."

Bakari escorted Anne and Alex to the artifact room. The dodecahedron sat in the middle of the room with the gemstone tablets jutting out around its circumference like five wings. Paintings, covered with tarps, leaned against the walls. They carefully began uncovering paintings, searching for Lady Brunel.

"Here's your dream-painting," Bakari announced.

Anne gazed at it longingly. She turned away and whispered, "Sorry, Mom, I'll look for clues right after I visit Lady Brunel."

"Found her," Alex said, folding up a tarp.

"You're sure about this?" Bakari asked Anne.

"Yes, Henhenet's water is amazing. I can't remember the last time I felt this strong." Anne grabbed Alex's arm and landed them in Lady Brunel's painting. Alex explained his tablet-rubbing theory to Lady Brunel.

"Finally! Something new!" Lady Brunel's eyes sparkled her excitement.

"So, can we make it onto the boat a few minutes sooner?" Alex asked.

"I gave up trying years ago," Lady Brunel responded, smiling. "It is time to try again. We can always jump back here if the sea gets too rough. But you must be with Anne to return," she added gravely.

"What exactly are you saying?" Anne asked.

"If you return without Alex, we will have a devil of a time finding him in those waves. Isadora lost Hubert in Antarctica once. It took us a day to locate him. Isadora was a neurotic mess, but Hubert loved the adventure." She laughed. "He said it was the best vacation — ever. No one but Isadora visited me after that."

"Isadora is planning to retire you," Anne said.

"I know, dear. It is a twelve-step process. Step one: distance the subject from her world." She nodded toward the blackened spot where *The Plexian's Plot* had hung. "I've had a good life."

"Don't give up yet. When Mom is back, she'll find a solution," Anne insisted.

"Don't make promises you can't keep." Lady Brunel smiled, resigned to her fate. "Now, before my pigments deteriorate further, let's have one last adventure. We need to enter Dumont's memory earlier. This time land exactly there." Lady Brunel pointed to the center mast. "Picture yourself holding the rope when you land or you will wash overboard. I will land here, behind the mast."

Lady Brunel opened the painting and time flashed by. She slowed, fixing on the right point. They jumped. Anne grabbed hold of the rope and Alex held tightly to her waist. Although the wind and rain stung his face, the boat felt stable.

"Let go of the rope," Alex said. "We can make it to the lower deck if we move fast."

"No! Keep hold!" Lady Brunel shouted. "Here it comes!"

A huge wave crashed over them, washing the deck and everything on it against the far side. Anne grabbed Alex's ankle as they tumbled over the side of the boat. Another wave loomed above them. Anne pictured Lady Brunel's portrait.

"Why did you bring us back here?" Alex snarled in frustration.

Anne snapped back. "We nearly died!"

Lady Brunel popped back into her painting. "I said it would be difficult."

"You mean impossible," Anne grumbled.

"What if we get on board a little sooner?" Alex suggested.

"It wasn't too bad until the big wave hit. With a few extra seconds, we could get below."

"That was one of many waves, and one of the longest breaks. The storm lasted three days. To avoid it, you would have to sit in the hold for almost two days. And that is real time for you," Lady Brunel said.

"We don't have two days," Alex complained.

Anne asked Lady Brunel. "Can you do it faster? You could wait in the hold and then come back and tell us what happened."

"Seeing the entire tablet would be worth the tedium of sitting in the hold, but I don't know the script language, and I have no way to record it. I cannot create new things in my world, just see and share what is already here."

Alex, determined to get aboard, studied the painting. "What if we wait until the ship rolls on its side — right after the wave hits — and target the open hatch that leads below deck."

"A direct shot inside?" Anne exclaimed. "You're nuts!"

"Don't you see? The ladder will be on its side. We just need to grab one of the rungs and swing our feet into position before the boat rocks back," he explained, his excitement mounting.

"The timing will need to be exact," Lady Brunel said, "and the hatch is too small for all three of us to make it safely below deck. The two of you might make it. To think, after all the years I have traveled in Dumont's paintings, I will miss the grandest adventure . . . ." She sighed. "Very well, I will open the time-window, you jump below, and I will land behind these large crates. They will keep me on board long enough to return. Then you are on your own. Your timeline will move forward parallel to mine. When you leave, you must exit my painting completely. Don't try to return to me. You could end up in the Void — or worse."

Lady Brunel opened the window into time, and they jumped. Anne landed them with a thump against the wooden ladder. Alex fumbled for a grip and lost sight of Anne. "Anne?" he shouted. Anne grabbed his wrist and pulled him across the ladder and onto the lower deck. The boat tipped back, and salty foam slammed them against the far wall.

The ship pitched again as another wave crashed across the deck. Alex found a rope and secured one end to a bunk. As more waves washed over the ship, they swung, but mostly hung from the rope. During the short spans between crashing waves, they inched toward the storage hatch. Finally, Alex threw the hatch open and pulled Anne inside. They sat in silence, shivering in the dark, waiting for Dumont. More than an hour passed before he arrived carrying a lamp and a roll of fabric.

Alex crouched next to Dumont watching him rub the tablet. For a split second, the pattern emerged on the cloth. The symbols were vivid before blurring. Alex restlessly waited as Dumont's hand moved toward the bottom corner. He was afraid to blink for fear of missing the message.

"Oh, my God. Energy matter lit by vibrating threads."

"Alex, what does that mean?"

"We have to get back to the Tablet Complex. Now!"

Anne grabbed his arm to return, but Lady Brunel's painting was gone.

CHAPTER EIGHTEEN

TIME LAG

Anne stared at the edge of the Void. "Oh, no! How could I make such a stupid mistake? I'm so sorry." Lady Brunel told her not to return to her painting, but Anne felt Alex's anxiety about the tablet.

Alex swayed. "Take us back. Something feels wrong — really wrong! Please hurry!"

Anne's body vibrated. The cacophony of sounds blared, as they had the first time Anne traveled with Aunt Margaret. "Don't let go, no matter what!" As lightning split the void, space spun into a kaleidoscope.

Instead of time waves crashing over them, Anne and Alex

tumbled into a wormhole. Worse than any manmade roller-coaster, the tunnel twisted, dipped and turned in random directions. Afraid she would soon pass out, she tried to picture the meditation room. No portal appeared. She knew she was risking a dimension breach inside the void, but she was running out of options. She reached for her pocket. The worm hole spun and dropped them into a free-fall. She almost lost her grip on Alex. "I can't hold onto you and reach into my pocket at the same time! Grab the bracelet and put it on my wrist."

Alex, frightened beyond caring about the personal space issues, dug his hand into her pocket and pulled out the bracelet. As he slipped it on her wrist, she felt, more than saw, shadows fluttering behind her. As the winged monster exploded through the wall of the wormhole, Anne pictured the dodecahedron, and a portal opened to the artifact room. She pulled Alex through and quickly closed the portal, locking the beast on the other side. Earth's gravity took hold of Alex. She couldn't keep her grip and dropped him on the floor next to Bakari.

"Anne, what's happening to you?" Bakari asked, watching Anne float above the dodecahedron.

"The dodecahedron's a doorway. It connects everything!" Anne proclaimed, and she knew — without doubt — she was a Demagogue. Golden light flashed against the walls as the dodecahedron opened. Anne disappeared.

"No!" Alex exclaimed. "It's happened . . . . I thought we would have more time . . . . Last time she stayed outside the dodecahedron . . . . She's alone . . . . I can't do anything to stop them!" Alex pounded his fists against the dodecahedron.

Bakari pulled him away from the dodecahedron. "Tell me what you think is happening."

Alex slumped to the floor. "Anne's fighting the Plexians. I shouldn't have let her put on the bracelet. It opened the dodecahedron just like Enheduanna's. Anne doesn't have Bruegel's ball. She's not prepared. She doesn't stand a chance. I've done it again. I am letting Anne die."

From inside the dodecahedron, Anne watched Bakari console Alex. She pushed her hands against the golden walls. I'm still alive — at least I think I am. An orange-tinged fog swirled around her and obscured her view of the tablet room. She felt an electric charge flow through her as bolts of energy jagged around her. Her eyes strained against the sudden flashes.

When the fog lifted, she fell, and the ground rose quickly to meet her. She landed with a thud and bounced off the spongy turf. Yuck! Anne thought, as she spit out the sour-tasting dirt. She tried to stand, but could not keep her balance. The ground popped and jumped like the surface of a pond during a torrential downpour, splashing debris high above her head. She dug her fingers into the squishy soil for stability. Hundreds of thread-thin, blue vines curled around her hands. The tendrils spiraled up her body, and her arms began to fluoresce, shifting from blue to gold. Anne tore free, but the damage was done.

"What's happening to me?" she shrieked, as the fluorescent colors bled into her skin. The popping ground settled and then slowly fell away as a massive mound of matter swelled in front of her. Covering the mound were swirling mosaics of windows into time.

"I'm in the Plexus! And that time wave is heading this way," she said aloud. She knew she should be thrilled to be the first to reach the Plexus, but sheer terror won. The time windows assaulted her senses. The shifting images made her dizzy, and the noises deafening. Worst of all, unlike traveling through paintings along the Void, the Plexus reeked like a garbage dump in the summer, covered in cherry jam. Anne fell to her knees, about to retch, but even throwing up would have to wait. Hundreds of fluorescent creatures swarmed down the hill toward Anne. Behind her, the ground split, and scores of giant blue tentacles surged from the depths of an abyss. Terrified, Anne dodged her way past the throng of creatures, now tumbling down the hill. She reached the top of the wave as it began to roll, and rode it to safety. Looking down into the pit of tentacles, she watched as a giant silvery viperfish with glistening blue eyes lunged from the hole. Its retractable jaw opened, exposing thousands of needle teeth.

"The viperfish's maw! The jellyfish are coming! I have no idea what to do!" Anne yelled.

Instead of spewing jellyfish from its mouth, the viperfish gobbled down the fluorescent creatures. The rising wave lifted beyond the viperfish's reach. In the distance where the horizon met a blazing, liquid sky, huge energy spiders glided from wave to wave on lightning silk. The spiders fled from an oozing river. "It's the river from my dream!"

An explosion split the river and thousands of nearly-transparent energy ants charged from its depths. Some of the ants were stuck in ooze along the river's edge, frantically struggling to free their legs. A wave of dark green and silvery-gray slime drowned them. Unlike the spiders' graceful dance —skittering from wave crest to crest — the ants that escaped the ooze dodged and wove through the undulating terrain, somehow sensing how to navigate the ever-changing maze. Anne's wave sank, bucking as it gave itself back to the core of the Plexus.

An ooze-stained ant charged straight at her, bolts of light crackling from its mandibles. Anne ran, searching for another wave to ride, but she was no match for the ant's speed. It was almost on top of her when strings of light lifted her from the ant's pincers. Glowing strands entangled her. It was the energy spiders! High above the growing battle, she watched a legion of spiders conduct a counterstrike, capturing ants in their webs. The ants thrashed and gnawed at the webbing, but could not escape.

Anne felt more than heard the spiders cry, "Help us! Cure the Curse! Awaken the Primal Key."

She tried to move, but her limbs refused. Then dread filled Anne's heart. The dark-winged monster was flying directly toward her. It darted around the spiders, its sizzling blood-red eyes trained on Anne.

"Let me go," she pleaded. "That thing wants to kill me!"

The monster swooped toward Anne. She squeezed her eyes shut and waited for the impact. It never came. She opened one eye and squinted at the creature hovering in front of her. Its beating wings swayed her energy-web cocoon as it spoke in a deep penetrating voice — a voice she knew.

Kill You?
Not True!

"You're the one!" Anne exclaimed recognizing the Bat's voice. "When I was Enheduanna, you told me what to write on the dodecahedron."

Bright Hand Wings' head bobbed as he stretched a wing toward the oozing river carving its way through the Plexus.

Your skills I need
With utmost speed.
My name is Bright Hand Wings.
New hope your advent brings.
At last I can elucidate
To you our need — perhaps they'll wait.
If you will bring the Key and mend the tear,
Then in exchange, your earth the lords might spare.

"That's what you told Enheduanna, too," Anne said, trying to free her arms from the sticky webs. "It didn't work out so well for her. Why can't you just leave us, leave me, alone?"

Bright Hand Wings sneered, his eyes flashing red. He hissed:

My liminal world keeps universes from colliding.
Our space, that oozing earth-born blight is dividing.
Gravity Clans claim destroying earths is our best chance
To keep our dimensions out of The Great Expanse.
Gravity laws are strong,
But their method, this time, is wrong.
If the E.M. Clans' world is shaken.
The Ooze will awaken

And consume us all.
The Plexus, all dimensions, will fall.

An inverted whirlpool began to suck the liquid from the sky, forming a deep, black hole. Anne's web sac, pulled toward the gaping sky. Orange and blue billowy jellyfish floated near the edges of the whirlpool. Bright Hand Wings sizzled at the sight of them and shifted to shield Anne.

The Gravity Lords appear.
They know you're near.
Your methods and spheres they fear.

Anne didn't have Enheduanna's sphere. Even if she had the weapon, her arms were wrapped tightly to her sides. She tried to see around Bright Hand Wings, to gauge how much time she had left, but he was too big. Bright Hand Wings wrapped his wings around her webbed cocoon and they plummeted toward the spiking ground. Seconds before impact, he spread his wings and whizzed through the maze of time-waves. In time with his flapping wings, he said:

To achieve my mission,
I broke tradition.
If they knew
I helped you...

As Bright Hand Wings darted around, a geyser spewed sour

soil hundreds of feet into the air. Anne's stomach turned, threatening to empty. He veered toward the oozing river.

My plan the Gravity Lords refuse,
But I must save my home from Ooze.
Now it's Gravity versus E.M. and Strings.
A coup, I hope, our defiance brings.
The Demagogue I help once more,
This time I risk a civil war.
Go to the Nazca Lines at night.
Mend Seth's hole and stop our plight.

A Gravity Lord spotted Anne and gushed liquid sky toward her. Bright Hand Wings dodged the blast.

The Gravity Lords now know.
You must go.

He severed the spider's web with his claw and dropped Anne. She plunged toward the ground.

"I'm going to die!" Anne screamed. A hole opened in a time wave as a viperfish rocketed out — swallowing her. She crashed through layers of meshed energy strings lining the creatures throat, pulling and kicking them aside until the orange fog returned. Inside the creature's belly, the dodecahedron floated toward her. The fog began to dissipate, and she landed in a heap on the artifact room floor.

She heard Alex's voice. "Anne . . . Anne, you can't die."

"I'm okay!" she tried to call out, but her words did not form.

She didn't feel hurt. Actually, she felt nothing, not even the floor beneath her.

Bakari knelt and checked her pulse. "It's really fast!" he said and started pressing her fingers. "Her skin is gray, and her fingernails aren't retaining color. She's in shock! Get something soft to put under her legs!"

Alex handed Bakari the tarp that had covered Lady Brunel's portrait. Bakari gently placed Anne's legs on top of it. She felt nothing.

"She has minor burns and cuts. Keep her warm," Bakari said. He grabbed a first-aid kit from the cabinet and began cleaning and bandaging Anne.

"What would make her so lifeless?" Alex asked. "It's like she's not really here."

Bakari gasped. "Time lag. SANDY, find Helena. I need her — now." Bakari placed a steadying hand on Alex's shoulder. "Anne's been to the Plexus. The Crystal Tablet warns that, if a human travels to the Plexus and doesn't adapt, time lag sets in."

"Is it deadly? Will she recover?" Alex asked, not caring if Bakari noticed his tears.

"It's best to wait and see if time catches up with her. If she has to, Helena will administer an aging potion."

Anne glared at the dodecahedron and wished she had never found it. The edges glowed as the winged creature hovered inside.

"What did you do to me?" Anne yelled, but her mouth refused to move. Bright Hand Wings heard her thoughts and replied:

Your body did not acquiesce,
And then it went through great distress.

"No kidding and now I can't move!" Anne snapped.

Agitated, Bright Hand Wings stretched his wings. Energy bolts from his pointy fingers ricocheted off the dodecahedron.

> We tried to help you to adapt.
> Within the Coupling, you were wrapped.
> Before it finished, you pulled free.
> A foolish move, you must agree.

"That viperfish ate me!"

Bright Hand Wings grabbed the dodecahedron with his thumb and crawled to the top. His eyes pulsated, brightening with each beat.

> You will get your movement back
> When your time is back on track.
> Some of you still lags behind.
> When it falls, you'll be combined.

Bright Hand Wings calmed his wings, hanging upside down to roost.

> Stop Seth's quaking
> To keep the E.M. realm from shaking.
> Before the Gravity Lords appear,
> Mend both tears with Bruegel's sphere.

His voice grew faint and his sizzling wings dimmed. Anne began to hear Alex and Bakari again. Helena had joined them.

". . . into the Plexus! You're certain?" Helena asked.

"No, but what else . . ." Bakari's voice faded.

Anne's stomach lurched. She was falling again. Her body crashed on the floor, knocking the air from her lungs. She could feel again! She tried to speak, but her mouth remained frozen. *Time is catching up with me. The rest of me just landed in the tablet room.* Her muscles cramped, and her head pounded. It wasn't long before Alex and Bakari realized Anne was moving.

"This will take her out of lag, but it won't be pretty." Helena gently dripped a dark purple liquid into Anne's mouth. It warmed her throat, and her heart pounded faster, pulsing blood into her limbs. Then her brain fogged. "She's coming around." Helena said.

Alex gathered Anne in his arms. She grunted and threw up.

"Thank God," Helena sighed. "That's a good sign. Aging tonics are so unpredictable."

"I kinda feel my hands again," Anne slurred as she wiped the vomit from her lips. She stiffened and hugged her arms across her chest. Her entire body prickled with pins and needles. She moaned as Alex laid her head on his lap. As Alex wiped the tears from Anne's cheeks, she whispered, "My winged monster saved me."

Slowly, the tonic cleared from Anne's brain and she could remember Bright Hand Wings' message. Adrenaline surged through her body. Ignoring the pain, she sat up. She set her jaw as she said, "Seth's using two spheres this time. He's going to blow a hole through the Nazca Lines and Mom." She wanted to act, but she sank back against Alex, exhausted.

MATTHEW CLARKE'S "KINDERSPIELE" MAP.

CHAPTER NINETEEN

𒀀𒉿𒌋𒁲𒐈

KINDERSPIELE

Anne dreamed she was snuggling her Fosby Bear, curled under her comforter in Collinsville, but she awoke on a make-shift hospital bed in Helena's triage center. She rolled onto her side and swung her legs over the edge of the bed.

Helena, who was inventorying medical supplies, turned and smiled. "Glad to see you're conscious. I must admit, I was concerned. You reacted poorly to the aging potion. On a scale of one to ten, what's your pain level?"

Anne considered her question. "Stiff back is a four, dull headache a three and neck blisters about a two." Her stomach grumbled. "I've starving. How long have I been here?"

"All night. It's nearly ten in the morning. Eat these." Helena pulled a bag from her medical bag. "If they stay down, you can move on to something more appetizing."

Anne opened the bag and took a sniff. They looked and smelled like Ritz Crackers, but she knew they were laced with a potion — probably cow lungs, or pig intestines or horse urine. She cautiously nibbled around the edge.

"I'll let Alex know you're awake." Helena typed a message into her comm-pad. "After you finish your snack, he can escort you to the meditation room. Isadora's eager to hear the details of your Plexian adventure. It's quite an accomplishment. The other Transcenders are positively green with envy — especially Abigail. She claims you hallucinated the entire thing."

"It was real," Anne said, more to convince herself than Helena.

"Of course it was! Alex told me the dodecahedron swallowed you up, and I know time-lag when I see it." She returned to her inventory, leaving Anne to finish her crackers and sip iced water.

Alex, with Bakari in tow, rushed into the triage center, both of them out of breath. "You're not . . ." Alex took a gulp of air. "getting out of my sight . . . until this whole thing is over."

Anne allowed Alex to help her stand. The blood rushed from her head; her vision blurred. No passing out, she told herself. She held onto Alex until the room came back into focus. Even with Alex's help, the walk to the meditation room (now the strike team's command center) sapped Anne's energy. The room bustled. Conversations overlapped as each team finalized its role in the strike. The loudest debate centered around the force of the hurricane Marcus planned to conjure up. As the team noticed her arrival, discussions died down — all eyes locked on Anne.

Everyone remained silent, waiting for Anne to recount her encounter with the Plexus.

Still unsteady, she sat in the nearest chair. "Seth's experiments cause earthquakes here, but in the Plexus they created a putrid, oozing river that is ripping through the E.M. clans' world. The Gravity Lords think destroying Earth in all parallel dimensions is the only way to stop the ooze from spreading into their realm."

Anne paused, expecting Abigail to scoff at the idea. Instead she paled.

"Enheduanna's sphere, can it stop them?" Isadora asked.

Anne felt Marcus probing her thoughts. She was too exhausted to stop him. She took a deep breath before continuing. "Not this time. The Gravity Lords know about me. I won't be able to get the sphere near them. Bright Hand Wings (the Bat) believes the Gravity Lords' plan will not only destroy Earth, but the Plexus as well."

"A Big Crunch," Selena said. "The universe will reverse direction, collapsing on itself, creating the next Big Bang."

Anne nodded. "We must return the Primal Key and figure out a way to close the tear in the Plexus. If Seth causes another quake and the E.M. world falls, the Gravity Lords will kill us."

Marcus stopped probing Anne's mind, convinced her trip to the Plexus was real. "Our plan doesn't change," he said definitively. "If we stop Seth, the Gravity Lords will leave us alone."

"It's not that simple," Anne persisted. "The Gravity Lords won't be satisfied until the oozing river completely vanishes."

"Inform Estrella of this development," Isadora told Abigail.

"Tell her I will join her in Nazca after the strike —"

"That's where the Primal Key is hidden," Alex interrupted her. "I've been studying the rest of the Carnelian Tablet. I think the Key is inside the Nazca spider. There are also instructions for using the spheres. The last line says energy matter lit by vibrating threads will seal time-tears and the Key locks it tight."

Isadora regarded Alex for a moment. "And you know how to create these vibrating threads?"

"Well, no, but —" Alex felt his face tighten and ears redden.

"Emma's initial translation differs from yours. It may take years to interpret the tablet correctly. Marcus, assemble your strike team," Isadora said and strode out of the room.

"Alex," Anne whispered. "Do you really think you know how to seal a time-tear?"

Alex's looked at the floor. "Isadora's right. I don't know how to light the energy matter or even if the Key is in Nazca. The tablet says to create a giant spider made of stones. In its belly you'll awaken the Key."

The command center was buzzing again. Attacking Seth was top priority. Everyone knew their role. Even George helped with the attack plans. Anne couldn't sit by doing nothing. "After I eat breakfast, I'm going into my dream-painting to figure out what "ect Greek Island" means. Want to come with?" If no one else would try to find Mom, she would.

"Of course. I told you, you're not allowed out of my sight."

Anne and Alex slipped out of the room unnoticed. It took two bowls of cereal and a banana, washed down by three glasses of orange juice, before Anne's stomach felt happy. While she stuffed her face, Alex shared his translation of the Carnelian

Tablet symbols. "The sphere design depends on the dimension it influences — ten spheres, two each for the each of the Plexian chief clans. They all rip time — safely — if used correctly." He pulled a scrap of paper from his pocket. "While you were recovering from time-lag, I came up with this.

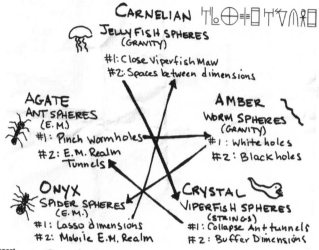

"Why is Grandpa's antique-antenna-key in the corner?"

Alex rolled his eyes. "Do you know what the symbols mean, and I don't mean your hamburger-man version."

Anne fidgeted in her chair. She never bothered to learn the ancient scripts. Why should she? The tablets were Alex's thing.

"The central symbols ⊤⌐⊕⧧☐⊤⋎⋀⅏⊟ on the Carnelian tablet are in Linear B script. They mean 'Vibrating Strings.' The recipe for energy matter is on the Amber Tablet. I always assumed the missing Carnelian symbols would explain how to create and use the vibrating threads — no such luck."

"Maybe you don't make them. They might just exist somewhere," Anne suggested.

Alex didn't acknowledge her idea. He tapped his pen on the worm spheres. "Right after I left my meld with Bruegel, my time shattered. I saw Lamia with the worm-sphere in the tunnel from your dream. If that's accurate, we need the correct ant-sphere to shut down Seth's experiment."

Anne stood, stretching her back. "Time to take a tour of dream-painting. We can't rescue Mom and stop the worm-sphere unless we know where they are."

Anne led the way to the artifact room to enter the painting she created of her dream. Alex propped it against the wall. Anne scanned the collage of images covering the canvas. "We're not going there." She pointed to the lower right corner, where translucent spiders mended their webs. The winged beast (she now knew as Bright Hand Wings) spun out of control. Anne remembered the pain as the flames consumed her. It was bad enough to dream such a fate. She never wanted to experience it in real life. She studied the three other scenes. "Your pick. Red-brown, rocky ground with a chasm leading to the Earth's core, building and tunnel ruins or the tunnel where Seth's keeping Mom?"

"Definitely the tunnel." Alex quickly answered.

Anne landed them near the crate that blocked the "ect Greek Island" message. The air tasted stale — like the tunnel had been sealed for years.

Alex tried to move the crate. It wouldn't budge. "What's in this thing?" he asked.

Anne shrugged. "I didn't open it during my dream."

"Then why did you paint it so heavy?" he complained.

Anne walked the length of the tunnel past more crates until

she reached Mom's discarded sandwich and water bottle. A locked, steel door big enough to drive a truck through sealed the end of the tunnel. "There's nothing here," she called back to Alex. "Let's try the ruins."

Anne and Alex landed in the collapsed tunnel. A breeze blew through the partial ceiling. Anne stared at the mound of stones, remembering the earthquake that caused the cave in. Somewhere under the rubble was Mom. Anne scrambled up the rocks and out into the misty, foggy night. As they searched the ruins of the Federal Style building, white debris showered them. The structure was deteriorating. Near what was once the building's grand entrance, Alex found a scrap of cloth. A ribbon of blue edged a filthy white background. In the center was a tattered West Virginia coat of arms. The ground shook and the remains of the building toppled. As sand covered with red-brown rock buried the grass, Anne pulled Alex back into the artifact room.

He reached for his CyberNexus and entered, "West Virginia Greek Island."

"That makes no sense," Anne said, but his search brought back an answer.

Alex read, "Project Greek Island. The secret congressional bunker discovered at the Greenbrier hotel. Mom's in West Virginia."

"We found her!" Anne exclaimed, hugging Alex so hard he dropped his CyberNexus.

"Now, let's get her back," Alex said, wiggling out of Anne's arms. "SANDY find Marcus."

"Marcus and the strike team left fifteen minutes ago," SANDY replied.

"Where's Isadora?" Anne asked, her excitement growing. If they could reach the bunker in time they could stop Seth's sphere and save Mom. Isadora would know how to disarm it.

"Isadora left the estate five minutes ago."

"Who's still here?" Alex asked.

"The students are in the tablet wings until the strike is completed," SANDY reported. "Helena is in the triage center and Selena is in the command center."

Alex dashed to retrieve Bruegel's sphere; Anne sprinted to the command center. Although tired and battered from her trip into the Plexus, her adrenaline kicked in, giving a burst of energy. She found Selena monitoring a six-foot, square screen covering the wall where the family portraits had hung. Red blips, marking the strike team members' progress, converged on Seth's command center. Across the bottom of a screen a message bar blinked, "maintain radio silence."

"We found —"

"Not now," Selena scolded. She pressed a button on her comm-pad and a weather radar map appeared in the top corner of the screen. "Marcus's hurricane is forming." Within minutes the strike team and Seth's command center were in the eye of a category one storm. Satisfied they were contained, Selena turned to Anne. "Phase one is complete."

"We found Mom," Anne blurted out, bouncing with delight. "If Isadora can get to West Virginia —"

"Isadora's inside *Kinderspiele* monitoring Seth's response to the strike," Selena explained. "She isn't planning to return until phase two is complete."

"Then I'm go into *Kinderspiele* to get Isadora myself." Anne stomped her foot. She had spent hours studying Dad's journal about the painting and knew she could navigate the maze.

To her surprise Selena didn't object. Instead she asked Helena to report to the command center. "Just in case you feel a bit spent when you return," she explained. She pulled up an image on her comm-pad and handed it to Anne. "That's Bruegel's *Big Fish Eat Little Fish*, the etching hanging in Seth's Command Center."

Anne looked at the disturbing scene. An enormous, beached fish belched smaller, human-sized fish from its mouth. A man, no taller than the fish's tail, sliced open its belly, spilling more creatures on the shore. In the foreground, a man and a little boy watched from a row boat. "What do you think that guy is telling the kid?"

"Big fish eat little fish," Selena replied. "In our world, the powerful instinctively prey on the weak. You can see why Seth likes this piece."

Anne wrinkled her face in disgust. "Is this etching alive?" She imagined the stench.

Amused, Selena smiled. "It can't be too bad. Bixia's spent hours inside it and she's a vegan." She pointed to the hill behind the fish. "Isadora always lands near that tree. You should land by the water next to the row boat. Isadora will see you once you scan forward to current time."

Anne nodded her understanding. "Dad said Bruegel's bonfire works like Aunt Margaret's."

"Bixia claims it's a smoother ride, but you still must move quickly when the time-stream opens."

"Or fall — forever — into the Expanse," Anne remembered

Isadora's self-portrait's words. She took a step toward *Kinderspiele*.

Selena blocked her way. "Remember, don't touch the toys inside that painting," she warned. "Don't speak. Don't even think about what you see." She paused, her hand clutching the black cloth. "Are you certain you have the path memorized? You can't stray or the kids will lure you into their games."

Anne slipped on the bracelet. "I'm ready." She said more confidently than she felt.

Selena removed the cloth. For Anne, *Kinderspiele* came to life. She focused on the bottom right corner and jumped into the scene.

Anne landed in front of the girl selling brick dust. Anne pressed her back against the wall to avoid a boy and a girl whizzing by, rolling wooden hoops with sticks. She stepped into the street, carefully avoiding a group of boys, rough-housing. In front of her, a girl blew into a pig's bladder trying to make a balloon. Even though she read about this game in Dad's journal, watching the girl puffing away gave her a chill. She stared at her a moment too long. The girl looked up and cocked her head at Anne. Anne felt a force pull her toward the girl. I'm going to become part of this game! I can't — it's too disgusting. Clear your mind, Anne told herself. You're invisible. The girl blinked a few times and returned to her smelly endeavor.

Anne dodged two boys rolling on a large barrel and stopped short as a game of leapfrog bounced in front of her. Anne watched in horror as the leap-frogger landed near six kids. They grabbed his arms and legs, swinging him over a wooden beam. Anne turned away to scan the crowded street before the boy's butt hit the board. Kids swarmed in every direction. Beyond the sea of kids, a river and country fields looked inviting. Laughter flowed from the games near the river, while the games played in the city streets caused yells, shouts, and tears. Anne knew the jump-off point was up the street, but the allure of the river enchanted her. She took a step toward the water. A tug-of-war match abruptly shifted direction, toward her. She jumped back to avoid the boy who toppled near her feet. I almost blew it, Anne realized. Stay on the path, she reminded herself.

She dashed between the leap-froggers, intending to reach the boy on stilts, but a group of boys and girls threw their hats at her head. She slid face first onto the ground to avoid them. Anne crawled then scrambled to a shop on the right side of the street — the wrong side according to Dad's map. In front of her, the road bustled; kids bowled, wrestled, spun in circles and chased each other. She found the next stop on the path. This one must be precise, she reminded herself. She had to pass the alleyway to reach the hide-and-seek game across the street.

In the middle of the commotion, Anne noticed kids playing a quiet game of marbles and hurried toward them. Two kids holding a chain crossed her path. "Chain the devil! Chain all the devils!" they yelled. The kids near them screamed and ran away. In seconds, the chain would hit Anne's stomach. She twisted to her right and sprinted past the marble players just before the chain wielders toppled them to the ground. A gap opened, and Anne darted up the road to the alleyway. A whirlpool of light and sour Plexian dirt swirled into the ground. A boy teetered near the edge about to topple inside. Anne's heart ached to help him. Not just him, she realized. A girl — Bridget — half stuck in the whirlpool, grabbed the back of the boy's shirt. He leaned forward, his knees almost touching the ground and pulled with all his might. He broke free, dragging a chain of kids behind him. Anne pressed against a building as they rushed past her. She wished she could grab Bridget's arm and break her bondage; instead she averted her eyes. They plowed onto the main street, cutting through the chain-the-devil players. A brawl erupted. Anne used the diversion to reach the hide-and-seek game.

The next games were less fierce. Kids played "who has the ball?" and gave piggyback rides. There was even a group singing door-to-door. As Anne neared the bonfire, she heard the burning wood crackling. Bright-colored embers shot into the air. The boys whooped with joy as the fire consumed Bruegel's works sending more embers skyward. As Anne slipped into the flames, the anarchy of *Kinderspiele* disappeared. Unlike the twisting kaleidoscope of paintings in Margaret's fire, Bruegel's paintings turned, like a carousel, around her. The narrow time-stream cut through the fire, separating Anne from Bruegel's masterpieces. *Big Fish Eat Little Fish*, passed her, too quickly, for her to lock onto her landing point. The stream widened. Time to jump, Anne told herself. Paintings spun past her. As the big fish came into view again, she focused on the rowboat and jumped.

She touched down on the beach, relieved nothing moved. Bruegel used ordinary pigments. Nothing could live here. She scanned forward from the 1500's, when Bruegel created the hub, to her current time. Moments after she arrived, Isadora made her way down the hill to join her. Isadora placed her index finger to her lips reminding Anne to remain silent. Anne pulled Isadora's sleeve, hoping she would understand they needed to leave — now. Isadora shook her head and pointed out of the etching into

216

Seth's command center. From Anne's vantage point, an electronic map of the world dominated the view.

On the top corner of the map, Lamia's face stared at her. "Sphere #1 is in Peru. I placed its mate with Elizabeth this morning." Lamia laughed cruelly. "She's keeping it company until we blow-up the bunker."

Anne sneered and clenched her hands. She hated this woman.

"What about the other spheres?" a man asked. He walked in front of the painting, temporarily blocking Anne's view. Anne's heart pounded as she looked at the back of the man she knew must be Seth. She glared at his short, white hair that didn't quite cover the fleshy folds of his neck. Anne's body tensed. She wanted to jump out of the sketch and attack him.

"I can't break Elizabeth. She won't betray the Collective, but if Matthew sent Bruegel's spheres to her, they're buried in the house rubble," Lamia said. "If he still has them, they will remain with him in Bruegel's *Netherlandish Proverbs*. He's a permanent part of that painting now. Bruegel's painting's locks are nearly impossible to break."

"Matthew is contained. The ant-sphere won't counteract your worm-spheres," another man said, his voice weak and hopeless. "I can form the white and black holes, but I'm not sure our energy mesh can contain a Plexian being. The spiders are ruled by E.M. (Electro-Magnetic) laws they —"

"Spare me the physics lesson," Seth snapped. "Malcom, are you ready at the Nazca lines?"

"The spider trap is in place and we've invited a Collective Transcender to observe the experiment."

"Wonderful. Perhaps she will be more reasonable than

Elizabeth. Prepare to light up Nazca's spider. After I deal with Isadora's strike force, we will have no more barriers." Seth took a few steps forward and Anne could see the map again. Red ovals over Peru and West Virginia blinked. She also saw a gaunt man with matted brown hair chained to a chair. Anne recognized him. He controlled the meshed energy-bubble that trapped Anne the night Mom was abducted.

"Please, spare Elizabeth," the man begged. "I've done everything you've asked of me."

Isadora let out a gasp. "Gerald?"

Seth turned and glared at the etching. His lips tightened over his teeth into a smug smile. Anne knew he had heard Isadora. Isadora knew it, too. She was already opening the windows in time.

"Isadora?" Seth sang to the sketch. "I've been waiting a long time for you to show up in my etching. It's time for the big fish to eat." He reached in his pocket for his lighter and set the etching on fire.

As flames blistered the landscape, Anne frantically searched the windows back in time. She locked onto *Kinderspiele's* bonfire.

"Find my red door!" Isadora screamed, the flames from Seth's lighter consuming her. "It's in the embers!"

The boys tending the bonfire heard Isadora and began poking at her with sticks. Soon the painting would trap them in the bonfire — forever.

Anne shuffled the embers with her feet, revealing the red door from Isadora's self-portrait. She had only one shot to get this right. Anne imagined the door opening into Isadora's room with its chair and dying fire and jumped, dragging Isadora into her self-portrait. The flames followed them, setting the portrait on fire.

The painted version of Isadora quickly took stock of the situation. "Get Isadora back to the estate. Don't worry about me."

Isadora, engulfed in flames, materialized in the meditation room next to Anne.

Selena and Helena yanked a brocade curtain off the wall and pushed Isadora to the ground. After several rolls, they managed to extinguish the flames. Anne tossed a pitcher of water on Isadora's portrait, to dowse the fire, but the painting was beyond repair. The painted version of Isadora sacrificed herself for them.

Isadora motioned for Helena to come closer. "Estrella . . . the strike —" She coughed violently.

Helena handed her a cup. Drink this. You've inhaled poisonous smoke from the painting." Isadora drank and collapsed, motionless on the floor.

"Is she dead?" Anne exclaimed.

"A strong tranquilizer," Helena replied. "Her burns are extensive. SANDY, inform my Healers we have our first casualty."

Hearing the word casualty jolted Anne from the shock of the fire. "Seth was waiting for us, he knows about the strike team, and Dad . . ." Anne's resolve dissolved. Tears streamed down her cheeks.

"What about Dad?" Alex demanded.

Between sobs, she choked out, "He's alive. Imprisoned in a Bruegel painting."

The spider zoomorph (created between 500 B.C. and 500 A.D.) located in the Nazca Dessert, southern Peru.

CHAPTER TWENTY

WORMHOLES

"Dad's been in Bruegel's *Netherlandish Proverbs* for more than thirteen years. Can he survive that long?" Anne asked. She felt tears forming again, but she would not let them escape. She was afraid that if she gave in to this emotion, all the pain she had bottled up would surface.

"He will remain preserved as long as he stays in the painting," Helena said. "If he leaves, time will catch up with him." She pulled Isadora's gurney's side rails up, locking them in place. "I'll inform you if Isadora's condition changes." She wheeled Isadora's burned body out of the room.

"Anne, we'll organize a search for Matthew after we stop Seth," Selena promised.

"Seth knows about the strike force. They're walking into a trap! You must contact them! Now!"

Selena closed her eyes tight as she squeezed the bridge of her nose. "No. Marcus and Thomas have a number of tricks up their sleeves. Seth couldn't have anticipated all of them."

"But —"

"No!" Selena said, firmly. "We keep to our plan. Anything else would cause chaos. I want you to stay with the other students on the transportation level until the strike team returns."

Anne knew she couldn't change Selena's mind, but she wasn't going to sit this one out. She motioned for Alex to join her.

"Grandpa's friend, Gerald, is alive," she whispered. "He's Seth's prisoner. Seth is forcing him to use Bruegel's spheres."

"Then he's the Amalgamator who will cause death and destruction — not me." Alex said in relief.

"You were right. Seth is worried about an ant-sphere. Gerald thinks Dad took it into Bruegel's painting."

"There are two. One tunnels into the E.M. realm. The other pinches the wormhole apart. Let's hope Isadora's sphere is the right one. West Virginia doesn't need a *Kinderspiele-like* alleyway." Alex's eyes glazed over.

Anne recognized his empty stare. He was seeing the future.

"It's bad news," he said, and looked at the command center's screen. The red blips moved closer to the gate surrounding Seth's base. Three blips disappeared, the others scattered.

"Phase two is failing. Get to the transportation level — now!" Selena yelled.

Instead of going to the transportation level, Alex headed for the studios. "We have to stop Seth's experiment."

Anne ran after him. "But you don't know how to create the threads."

Alex raced through the studio and out the main door. "If Bright Hand Wings is on the up-and-up, the Gravity Lords will destroy us. If I can't fix the tear, and we're all going to die, I want to be with Mom," he said.

Tears streamed down Anne's cheeks as she followed Alex down the dark forest path. She wanted to be in Mom's arms in the worst way, but knew her fate, if Bright Hand Wings was right, would be settled at the Nazca lines. The road to the mansion was better lit and Alex increased his pace.

In his room, he grabbed his backpack, shoving his jacket, Bruegel's jellyfish-sphere and a bottle of water inside. He opened his Cyber-Nexus and sent George a message: "Operation Light-It-Up is a go. Isadora's office in five minutes."

From her room, Anne grabbed her jeans jacket and gently placed Fosby Bear on the pillow before leaving.

When they arrived in Isadora's office, Chasca crossed her arms and grinned at Alex. "You're about to get me in trouble again, aren't you?"

"Really, really big trouble this time." Alex agreed.

Only George knew the details of Alex's plan. Chasca, Bakari, and Olivia sat in stunned silence as he explained why and how he wanted to use the energy matter. "After we're off the estate, Olivia will tell Selena our plan. Bakari and George, you will wait at the shack for us to return." They both agreed. Alex turned to Chasca. "We need to get to the Greenbrier hotel in West Virginia."

"Does the Greenbrier have a museum?" Chasca asked.

Alex pulled out his CyberNexus to check. "There's something

called the Presidents' Cottage History Museum."

"That sounds important enough to be on Emma's list," she replied. "I'll drop you off, but if the world is going to implode, I'm going to Nazca to find Tia Estrella."

"How do we leave? The estate is locked down." Anne protested. "And what about the energy matter?"

Alex patted George's shoulder. "We've got that covered."

"And the pack?" Chasca asked nervously.

"I checked. SANDY locked the dogs down, too," George replied.

"So, who's going to grab the ant-sphere?" Alex asked.

Everyone looked at the bronze panther on the bookcase.

"Fine," Chasca complained. I'll sacrifice myself." Chasca looked from the panther to the sphere, timing her move. She grabbed the ball and the panther pounced. After knocking her hand against the shelf a half-dozen times, the panther released her, leaving ten paper-thin slashes on her wrist.

Using their CyberNexus screens as flashlights, they made their way through the swamp to Shades of Death River. When they reached the other side, Alex told George to take the others to his shack. In the moonlight Anne could make out Alex's silhouette as he pulled the water bottle out of his backpack and set it near a tree.

Bakari helped Anne navigate George's boardwalk and the climb up the rocky hill to the shack. Inside, George opened the cabinet and carefully removed a vacuum tube containing a lump of clay that looked like silly putty after someone pressed it across the Sunday comics.

"When Alex lights that stuff, what will happen?" Bakari asked.

"Alter or maybe even seal the tear — I hope, otherwise it will shoot magma up through the fractures. Nazca and the Greenbrier will become proud owners of their very own volcanoes."

"George, can you split the energy matter?" Anne asked.

George stared at her — puzzled.

"The tear won't seal permanently without the Primal Key. I'm going to find it."

George carefully split the energy matter and handed one tube to Anne. "Alex isn't going to like this."

"Like what?" Alex asked, joining them. He saw the energy matter in Anne's hand and unzipped his backpack. "I'd better hold on to that."

"I'm going to Nazca." Anne announced. "I'm planning to close that breach from the inside."

"The inside of what?" Alex asked.

"The spider."

Alex stomped his foot. "There's no way you're leaving my sight."

Anne couldn't help laughing. He looked just like Mom when she was angry. "You have to save Mom and I need to go to Peru to find the Key or your plan will fail — you know it will."

"I have to keep you safe this time. You might die without —"

"Every time I die you kill me — remember? Splitting up might be a good idea this time."

Alex turned away from her. George staggered backward, and Anne's heart paused, as they felt Alex's pain flood over them. The sadness, guilt, and shame from killing Anne so many times surfaced, leaving him raw inside. "I won't kill you this time," he whispered.

"I know you won't," Anne said gently.

"I'll go with her," Bakari offered.

George chuckled. "Count me in, but Olivia's going to kill us for leaving her behind."

"What about the Gravity Lords?" Alex asked, through clenched teeth.

Anne reached into Alex's backpack. "I'll bring Enheduanna's ball and the ant-sphere with me."

"Enheduanna died — remember!" Alex yelled.

Anne did remember. Every hour that passed she remembered more about her lives. "We don't have time to debate this," Anne said. "As soon as Seth stops the strike team, he'll use the spheres."

"You'll need this." Chasca transmitted a map of the Nazca Lines to Anne's CyberNexus. She zoomed in on the map and traced over the spider biomorph. "Tia Estrella believes the spider marks an entrance to the E.M. realm. To get to the spider, take the highway into the desert valley. There's an observation tower and a place to park along the road. From the tower you can see the huarango tree biomorph. Stand at its roots. From there your CyberNexus can guide you to the spider."

"We're driving?" George asked nervously.

"How far is the spider from the portal point?" Anne asked. "Can't we walk or take bikes?"

"In the desert?" Chasca asked, dismissing the idea. "Tia Estrella leaves a car parked just outside the museum's wall. One of you will have to drive."

"I can try," Bakari offered. "My dad sometimes lets me drive our tractor."

"Then we're set," Anne said.

Chasca pulled the team through George's portal.

Anne cringed as they landed in Emma's cramped, book-cluttered office. Less than a week ago, she woke up on the cot in the corner, still feeling the effects of the tranquilizer.

"This is Emma's portal," Chasca explained. "The office is shielded to hide the energy patterns, but from here you can reach every major museum in the world."

"And you know how to navigate it?" Bakari asked, skeptically.

"Let's just say I like taking exotic field trips," Chasca replied. "First stop, the Greenbrier."

They landed in the dark entry hall in the Presidents' Cottage.

"Find Mom," Anne pleaded.

"Don't die," Alex shouted back as he sprinted out the front door.

Chasca opened Emma's hub and jumped to Maria Reiche's garden in Peru. A white-and-red wall surrounded the museum that was once the archaeologist's home.

Anne pulled Chasca aside. "I need you to go back to the Greenbrier."

"But Tia —"

"Will live, we'll all live if this works. Alex might need a Transcender."

Chasca nodded. "Look for my tia."

"I will. Keep my brother out of trouble."

Chasca disappeared.

Outside the museum's main gate, as Chasca promised, an old car sat under a tree.

"Shotgun," Anne said, beating George to the front door.

George groaned and folded himself into the back seat while Bakari, the only one with any driving experience, started the engine. As he latched his seatbelt, he shifted uncomfortably. From his pocket he pulled a blue-green ceramic Bes statue. "I've been meaning to give this to you. It's a gift from Henhenet — kind of a mother-daughter protection thing."

Anne placed the Bes on the dashboard. "Let's hope it works."

Bakari fumbled with the clutch, lurching the car onto the Pan-American Highway.

"Looks like we're going the right way," George said, as they passed a worn sign that read, "LINEAS Y GEOGLIFOS DE NASCA."

The reddish-gray desert hills reminded Anne of pictures she had seen of Mars. Sand and stone cliffs cramped the road as it curved to the right. "It's like someone sliced through the hillside," Anne said as the walls of stones rose. "Can you speed up? We have to get to the observation tower before Seth's agents."

"I'm already going twenty over the speed limit," Bakari said and clutched the steering wheel tighter.

"Watch out!" George yelled, pointing out the front window. Two trucks, side-by-side, barreled toward them.

"Get off the road!"

"There's no room!"

"Turn around!"

"I can't!"

"Hit the brakes!" Anne shouted.

Bakari slammed the brakes. The steering wheel shimmied, and his arms shook.

"Drive into the hillside!" Anne yelled.

"We'll crash, and they'll broadside us!"

"Do it! Now!" Anne screamed and covered her eyes with her hands. She heard the blare of an air horn as one truck roared past them.

"Where did the other truck go?" Bakari asked, his voice quavering.

Anne's hands slid down her face. Bakari managed to stop the car half on and half off the road, inches from the hillside. "It worked! It actually worked!" she said and started to giggle.

Once they were moving again, and Anne calmed down, Bakari asked again, "Where did the truck go?"

Anne grinned. "Through a portal. I've only tried it with grapes. I wasn't sure it would work on something so big."

"You didn't send it to Isadora's meditation room, did you?" George asked. He sounded worried, but Anne heard him swallow a laugh.

"No, I dumped it into Aunt Margaret's lake."

"What about the driver?" Bakari asked.

"I don't know. I've never sent a person through a portal without an escort. I had my eyes closed. I hope I didn't break Bixia's first Portal Protocol and create another sloppy portal."

"Let's hope he can swim, and more importantly, Aunt Margaret forgives you for polluting her lake," George said.

When the road flattened, Anne spotted the observation tower. Bakari parked the car in a lot across the road. He pointed to a porta-potty in the corner of the lot. "Anyone need to go? Now's the time."

George got out of the car and sniffed the air. "I'll pass," he said and nodded toward the tower. "Do you think Seth's sphere is up there?"

"My guess is Seth's agent buried the sphere in the lines somewhere," Anne said as they crossed the road, "but we should check anyway."

Most of the vendors at the base of the tower had packed up for the day and were beginning to leave. A woman walked up to Anne. "American?" she asked. Anne nodded and hoped the woman wasn't going to try to sell her something. They didn't have the time for souvenir shopping. "Not safe for you. Leave now. Not safe at dark," she said. A man called out to the woman, and she hurried to join him on a motorcycle.

"She has no idea just how dangerous it's going to get tonight," George said as they climbed the three stories to the top of the tower.

"There's the huarango tree biomorph over there," Bakari said, pointing at the piles of rocks in the shape of a tree.

Anne heard a mechanical sound in the distance. "I think the sphere is about to arrive. I doubt that helicopter is bringing tourists to see the Nazca Lines."

Bakari grasped the railing. "I don't want to be up in this tower if the earthquake starts."

"Whoever's in that helicopter will see us," George said.

"They're about to rip open the earth. They won't care about a few kids in the desert," Anne replied.

As they hurried to the huarango tree's roots, Anne powered up her CyberNexus to check Chasca's map. "The spider biomorph isn't far."

The helicopter hovered over the Pan-American Highway and landed. Three armed men stepped out. A fourth dragged a woman in hand-cuffs onto the highway.

"That's Chasca's aunt," George said.

Seeing the kids, the three armed men sprinted toward them.

"Anne, go!" Bakari yelled. "We'll hold them as long as possible." Bakari disappeared into camouflage mode.

As Anne neared the spider, she ventured a look behind her. There was no sign of Bakari, which was good, but two men had captured George.

The third, only 50 yards behind her, shouted, "Stop, you'll be vaporized!"

Anne stumbled on the stone row and fell inside the spider glyph. Seth's spider trap activated. Electric blue bolts surrounded her in a meshed dome. Anne struggled to breathe as the oxygen was stripped from the air. In front of her sat a worm-sphere.

Seth's agent spoke into a comm-pad. "Isadora's a no show, but we have someone better — Anne. "Have Gerald change the modulations so I can release her."

The man collapsed, a dart sticking out of his neck. Bakari appeared next to him. "How do I shut the trap down," he asked.

"You can't." Anne rasped, pulling her bracelet out of her pocket. "Help George." Anne looked back toward the highway. "Or not." Bakari's assassin moves were impressive, but what George whipped up was truly inspired. As a dust storm raged down the hill toward the helicopter, Anne slipped on the bracelet and split the spider's abdomen. The worm-sphere activated.

If the Primal Key was ever inside the spider, it was now gone.

Seth's first fracture line sliced through the nothingness of the Void. The sphere created a swirling white hole. From its core, ribbons of light shot toward her. Not just light, Anne realized, matter and beings from the E.M. realm. The sphere from the Greenbrier bunker rocketed through the debris, yellow-hot, like a sun. It imploded creating a black hole that merged with the white hole, forming a wormhole. It sucked Anne inside.

Unlike the intense rollercoaster ride she experienced after leaving Lady Brunel's painting, this wormhole was ear-popping, pushing and pulling her in five directions at once. She flopped like a ragdoll. Just when she thought she would lose consciousness, the current stabilized. A large, black wing closed around her. Bright Hand Wings tightened his grip and pulled her toward his head. His red mouth opened. He's going to eat me! Anne tried to pull free. He clutched her tighter and yelled:

> The E.M. clans escaped,
> And in their wake a breach has shaped.
> You didn't mend the tears.
> Now the Ooze line flares.
> Why did you wait?
> It's now too late!

"What do you want from me? The Key wasn't inside the spider. Why do you have to speak in rhyming couplets? Just tell me what to do. By the way, your breath smells like burned fish!" Anne didn't know why she was attacking him personally, but it felt good.

Bright Hand Wings cocked his head. He curled his tail to his wing and grabbed her with his hind foot, his wings sizzling.

You think that my rhymes sound too trite.
I hope my new verse is all right.
I can broaden my range,
Although it feels strange
As it interferes with my flight.

"Stop! That's worse!" Anne screamed, as Bright Hand Wings bobbed awkwardly to the rhythm of his limerick.

Without another word, Bright Hand Wings flew straight through the side of the wormhole. A viperfish maw appeared and jellyfish Gravity Lords poured out if it.

"I'm ready!" Anne yelled, as she dangled behind him. With great effort, she pulled the jellyfish sphere from her pocket, holding it in front of her.

Bright Hand Wings sizzled a snarl, stopped short, and banked away from the Gravity Lords, yelling:

Enheduanna's sphere!
Lords don't come near!

"But I thought you wanted me to stop them. What else should I use?" Anne returned Enheduanna's sphere to her pocket and pulled out the energy matter and the ant-sphere for Bright Hand Wings to see.

Bright Hand Wings screeched:

You bring pure energy matter!
The Plexus, you'll shatter!

"Not if you tell me where to find the Key."

Bright Hand Wings hovered in place and folded his body until Anne faced him. His eyes blazed.

If you're ready to die,
The best way I'll supply.

He arched his back, stretched his wings and dove, dragging Anne back into the wormhole, speeding to the point where the white hole and black hole merged. As they neared the event horizon, the point in the black hole where the gravitational pull is greatest and escape is impossible, Bright Hand Wings' reared and hovered.

We still might avert the war
If the ant-sphere hits the core.
Drop it.
Stop it.

Bright Hand Wings flew through the event horizon. Anne waited until they reached the bright core of the white hole and threw the ant-sphere into it. An explosion bloomed, tearing the wormhole apart. The energy from the white hole whipped as a chain of explosions blasted their way toward the end of the ribbons of light. Unaffected, the black hole continued to suck in matter. Bright Hand Wings sped into the remains of the ribbons, emerging in the E.M. realm. He swooped across the growing river of ooze, accelerating as the ground spiked. A hole opened in a time wave. A viperfish lunged at them. Bright Hand Wings stopped short of the creature, cupped his wings and shot up to the sky.

Bold steps you take,
But are you awake?
The E.M. waves are the past.
But it will not last.
Through their sky your future waits.
Which future, your choice dictates.

Bright Hand Wings flew straight into the liquid sky, rowing his wings through the viscous fluid. Currents that led into the future streamed around Anne. Bright Hand Wings dipped inside one. Anne saw the strike team's future in the current. Seth's agents held Marcus, Thomas and Simon at gun point. Seth strode toward them, smashing cockroaches that coated his command center's floor. "I don't know how you sabotaged my experiment, but the black hole still stands. Your Elizabeth will die, sucked into its event horizon. Nothing can stop that now."

Seth's building shook as the hurricane's full force hit, knocking them to the floor. Seth sputtered, wiping smashed bugs from his face. "Shoot the boy first. Leave them for the roaches."

Anne jolted as Bright Hand Wings pulled away into a different current.

This flow contained a charred, lifeless landscape that made Anne feel hollow and ill. Bright Hand Wings must have sensed her sadness, because he quickly pulled her out of that current into a smaller eddy. Anne saw, at the bottom of it, George, Bakari and Estrella leading Seth's Nazca agents into the estate's swamp.

Bright Hand Wings thrust his wings again, flapping quickly to catch yet another tide. This time Anne saw the partial ruins of Greenbrier. Alex, Mom and Chasca emerged from the collapsed roof of the tunnel. "He did it! He got to her in time! The earth quaked, knocking them down. A chasm opened to the fiery abyss from her dream. Alex slipped toward the edge. Mom and Chasca grabbed his arms, stopping his slide. Alex's legs dangled over the edge, as Mom and Chasca tried to pull him to safety. He reached into his pocket for the energy matter. Chasca lost her hold on him. "Alex!" she screamed. He turned, looked at her, and dropped the vial. Anne watched, helplessly as they slipped into the chasm. Although she could not hear him, she saw him yell, "I'm sorry!"

Anne screamed. "No! Enough!" The current dissolved.

Bright Hand Wings spoke:

The Demagogue you are.
The Primal Key remains afar.
Now, which path will you take?
You know all that is at stake.

The Plexian sky had shown her the future, but she couldn't possibly save everyone. She might not be able to save anyone. What would Enheduanna do? She relaxed her mind and body, letting her past life experiences flood into her consciousness.

A new current arrived in the Plexian sky. It twisted and danced around the others. Anne thought she saw the owl that released her soul from the Labyrinth flying inside it. "Can I look inside that future?" she asked.

Bright Hand Wings sizzled anxiously.

> That current belongs to the Strings.
> It buffers all with threaded rings:
> A maze of infinite turns
> From which no one returns.
> Many try. None escape.
> Once inside, dimensions reshape.

"That's the one," she said, smiling at the owl.
Bright Hand Wings hesitated.

> Are you sure
> You can endure
> A string that pure?

"Yes, the Primal Key is now awake," Anne said firmly.

Bright Hand Wings accepted her answer. As they entered the chaotic current, a barrage of images, sound and smells assaulted her. The Universe's pasts, presents and futures assaulted her senses. Infinite strings spun like living whips of spaghetti from a dark hole that flashed in a Big Bang. "Which one is my reality?" Anne asked, scanning the spaghetti strands for a familiar image.

Bright Hand Wings tightened his wings into a shrug.

> I've never come inside
> For fear I might collide
> With a string and change its tide;
> Its unborn fate denied.

"You mean I could destroy a universe — my universe? Then take me back to the Plexus!"

Bright Hand Wings swooped to avoid the fast moving strings.

> That strand I lost
> When we crossed.

Anne closed her eyes to calm her thoughts. I need a focal point, she told herself, like scanning a painting. She recited one of Aunt Margaret's lessons. "All you have to do is focus on something on the other side of the window — a word, a texture or an object." She pictured Simon's face. "Shoot the boy first," Seth had said. Hundreds of spaghetti strings flowed around her, all with images of Seth, Simon and the roaches. "Which one?" she yelled. Her spirit owl grabbed a string in its beak and wound it around her.

Anne saw Seth's base swaying from the hurricane force winds Marcus conjured up. "Shoot," Seth insisted and his agent obliged. Anger swelled in Anne. She pictured Seth and his men, imagining their dead bodies decaying.

She yelled, "Rotting flesh!" The cockroaches attacked Seth and his agents, covering them until all Anne could see was a writhing mass of insects. "Save Simon," Anne said. Some of the roaches skittered away from Seth and slid under Simon. His limp body scooted across the floor. Anne wanted to stay and make sure they made it out, but she heard Alex call out, "I'm sorry!" from a single time string, whipping beneath her.

"Go!" Anne yelled to Bright Hand Wings, pointing at Alex's string. Instead of swooping around it, he dove inside and they emerged over the rising lava lake beneath the Greenbrier — the lava the ant-sphere explosion created. Anne looked up, searching for the owl. Far above her, Alex slipped over the edge. Mom and Chasca grabbed his arms, but they couldn't hold on for long. "Alex," she yelled, but any connection they had in the future-strings was severed. For a moment she closed her eyes to concentrate. She looked one last time in their direction. An air current swirled toward them as Alex's vial of energy matter fell past her. She watched as the vial reached the oozing river winding through the lava. It exploded. A geyser of ooze erupted, knocking Bright Hand Wings off balance. He screeched and spun out of control.

As they tumbled, Anne saw the owl, clutching time-strings in her beak, soaring over the river. "Let me go. I'm wide awake."

Bright Hand Wings dropped her. Clutching her energy matter, Anne plunged into the ooze; it consumed her.

CHAPTER TWENTY-ONE

THE PRIMAL KEY

Alex's legs dangled high above the growing lava lake. Stretched over the chasm's edge, Mom and Chasca strained to keep hold of him. Alex knew their strength was fading. He reached in his pocket for the vial of energy matter. He felt more than heard Anne call his name. Turning to find her he lost his grip on the vial. It tumbled toward the lava lake. His reality shattered. A single fracture line into the future jutted out before him. There was now only one way forward — one possible future. He watched the energy matter hit the lava and the winged creature drop Anne into the ooze. Alex knew the vial he just dropped would kill Anne. The time fracture ended and closed back to his present. Alex's heart pounded in his ears, drowning out everything else. "I'm sorry," he yelled.

"Alex, we need to go — now!" Chasca yelled. The ground shook and crumbled, dropping them over the edge.

Chasca focused on Anne's swirling air current. It crackled then split. Instead of lava, Alex plunged into cold, dark water. He didn't care. His body sank. He had failed. He had killed Anne — again. Chasca grabbed his arm and swam to the surface. His body instinctively pulled air into his lungs, but he didn't want to live. He didn't deserve to live. He kept seeing the vial explode and Anne fall into the ooze. He hated himself. Chasca swam to the side of the lake, pulling Alex with her. Mom helped them onto the beach and they dropped to the ground — exhausted. Alex crawled to his mother. She pulled him into a hug and he melted in her arms. "Mom . . . Anne . . . I . . . Sh-sh-she," he stammered.

"Shhh," Mom hushed, hugging him closer. "We'll find Anne."

She doesn't know, Alex realized. She didn't see Anne fall.

He swallowed his tears as Aunt Margaret hurried along the shore, an irate man trailing her shouting in Spanish. "Who's responsible for this . . . this . . . drunk? He drove his truck into my lake! I pulled him free, but Lord knows how I'm going to retrieve his vehicle." She saw Elizabeth. "OH! Thank God, you're safe."

While Elizabeth tried her best to explain what happened at the Greenbrier, Chasca briefly spoke with the man. "He's from Peru. He was delivering cola near the Nazca Lines when he landed here. The good news is he is still really drunk. If we get him back to Peru, he might think he hallucinated the whole thing. Anne must have sent him."

Alex winced at the mention of Anne's name. He wanted to blurt out the truth, but instead he withdrew deeper into dark thoughts.

"I knew Anne would bridge the physical and imagined planes!" Margaret said, doing a funny little victory dance. "I'm thrilled she managed such a large delivery, but really, did she have to pollute my lake? Once you get that driver home, ask Anne to stop by. I want to hear every lovely detail."

Alex couldn't bear it anymore. "Anne's dead! We didn't have the Key to close the tear. When I dropped the energy matter, she fell into the lava lake! The ooze swallowed her! Mom, I'm so sorry."

Elizabeth sank to the ground. "Anne traveled back in time. She told me about Seth's attack. I was so afraid I would ruin our future if I used the information. I've lost Matthew, now Anne."

Alex had never before seen such pain in her face. Margaret tried to console Elizabeth, tried to reassure her she was right to leave the future alone. Mom just shook her head. Alex sat next to her in silence.

The tears never came, but Mom's face turned stormy. She stood and brushed the sand from her pants. "Chasca, we better leave. We need to let the others know what happened."

Margaret regarded Alex, sadly. "Helena can give him something for the shock." She turned to Chasca. "And please, take this drunk out of here."

Chasca escorted them out of Margaret's painting into the artifact room.

"Alex, Chasca, and Elizabeth are in the complex," SANDY announced. "Security breach . . . security breach . . . unidentified man in the artifact room."

Olivia who was sitting near the tablets stood in surprise. "You made it!" Olivia pointed at the truck driver. "Who's he?"

Chasca explained the situation. Hearing the details sickened Alex again.

Olivia looked at the dodecahedron

"Selena wanted me to wait here, in case Anne . . . you know . . . made a grand entrance. I'm sorry," she told Alex. "What happened in Peru? Where are George and Bakari?"

"We don't know," Chasca said, "but I'm going to Nazca. I'll find them and take this drunk home."

Olivia's CyberNexus chimed. She checked the message and urgently said, "SANDY track George's comm-signal."

"George is on Bear Island in Wild Cat Swamp," SANDY reported.

"They're safe," Chasca sighed in relief.

Olivia held up her CyberNexus. "George sent me an S.O.S. — something is wrong."

"No one else is going to get hurt," Alex declared as he marched to the door.

"Alex, wait," Mom called after him. "You can't —"

Alex balled his hands into tight fists. "They're out there because they believed I could seal the breach. I must help them." He turned to Olivia. "Take Mom to the command center. Tell

243

Selena I'm going into the swamp. If the strike team returns, send —"

"I'm going with you" Olivia insisted.

Elizabeth stared into Alex's eyes — the look she used when there was bad news. Alex planted his feet firmly, holding her gaze. Finally, she nodded. "I'll tell Selena."

"She's in the meditation room," Alex said and raced from the room. Chasca and Olivia followed close behind him.

Hours earlier, when they left for the Greenbrier, the moon highlighted the path between Trout Creek and Shades of Death River. Now a fog, so dense Alex couldn't see the ground, enveloped them. To save time, Olivia insisted they take the direct route to Shades of Death River, jumping across the mounds of grass that dotted the swamp. Although she managed river currents with ease, blind navigation challenged her talents. More than once she missed her mark and Alex's sneaker disappeared with a slurp into the muck. Although it wasn't visible yet, Alex heard Shades of Death River.

A man yelled in the distance. "Clear up this fog or I'll shoot her!"

"Don't do it!" A woman insisted.

"Tia," Chasca gasped.

George didn't test the man's threat. The fog dissipated, forming a path between Bear Island and the river.

"We've got to get to the other side before they leave the boardwalk," Alex insisted.

Olivia quickly pulled the canoe to the river's edge. Alex kept his eyes on the boardwalk entrance as Olivia's oar pulled through ghostly faces in the river. When they landed, Alex jumped from the canoe and rushed to the large maple tree where he had stashed the bottle of water. He heard a splash and a man curse. Seth's agents were only minutes away from the river.

"Find a place to hide," Alex told the girls. He ran along the beach, whispering, "Edward. Edward Devillin." The malaria-ridden ghost appeared. "I can cure you and release your soul, but I need your help first." Alex quickly described his plan and then hid.

Seth's four agents from Nazca emerged from the swamp, holding George, Bakari and Estrella at gun point. As they reached the bank of the river, the ghosts attacked, possessing the agents. The men fell to the ground, writhing in pain.

"Tia," Chasca rushed to Estrella.

Olivia kissed George's cheek. His emotions leaked, but Alex didn't mind. For a moment he savored George's lighthearted excitement before returning his attention to Seth's agents. "Bakari, I need you," he called.

"What's wrong with them?" Bakari asked.

"Malaria." Alex passed the bottle of water to Bakari. "It's water from the Stela — enough for five. Heal them."

Bakari, as Horus, recited the spell Henhenet taught him. As the malaria symptoms weakened, all but one of the ghosts trapped in the river floated ashore. Seth's agents, still the 19th century ghosts, thanked Bakari and Alex profusely.

"There's one more," Alex said. "Edward Devillin." He moved to sit next to him on the river bank.

"I cannot ask you to suffer," Edward said, too pained to move.

Alex pointed to the river. "You must or your wife will remain in her watery grave."

Edward nodded, and possessed Alex. Together they screamed in pain. Although Bakari administered the water, it felt like hours before Alex-Edward could sit up. Edward released his body and joined his wife by the river.

"As soon as we get Seth's agents locked up, your souls are free," Alex told the ghosts.

Edward, his arm around his wife, said, "If it is not too much trouble, we would like to stay a while."

The wind picked up, blowing whips of fog across the river. Olivia punched George in the arm. "Stop messing with the weather."

"It's not me, honest," he protested.

On the other river bank, three men emerged from the mist — a swarm of mosquitos that moved like a black blizzard behind them.

"Dad, wait!" George yelled too late.

The mosquitos buzzed toward Seth's agents.

"Do something," Alex pleaded. If the ghosts leave their bodies —"

George reached out his hand. A frigid wind blew from Bear Island. As the mosquitos met the gale, they dropped like hail, skittering across the now frozen river. "Cold fronts have always been my strength," George smiled, confidently.

Leaving the river to thaw naturally, Marcus escorted them to the command center. Alex listened as he and Bixia debated how best to restrain Seth's agents. They settled on Lady Brunel's arctic adventure as a make-shift prison. As the ghosts released

Seth's agents, Helena sedated them so Bixia could safely transport them.

Most of the strike team members were undergoing treatment in the triage center — Simon the only critical patient and Anne the only casualty. The thought ripped Alex.

"You're certain Anne didn't survive the fall?" Marcus asked Elizabeth. "I felt her at Seth's base when Simon was shot. The roaches moved him to safety. I'm convinced she was behind it."

"I didn't see or feel her at the Greenbrier and Alex is convinced." Mom replied.

"At the Nazca Lines," Estrella reported, "the spider split and Anne disappeared. Seth's white hole spewed Plexian matter and energy spiders into some type of mesh trap. The earth quaked knocking us to the ground. Everything within 100 yards of the spider was sucked into the breach."

"Anne used the ant-sphere to pinch the wormhole," Alex said. "The white hole collapsed, but she needed the Key and the energy matter to seal the breach and close the black hole."

Estrella placed her hand on Alex's shoulder. "I'm so very sorry. I thought the spider was the Key. When Seth's agents realized the experiment failed, they forced us to bring them to the estate. Once they secured the Tablet Complex, Seth planned to steal the tablets."

"Where is Seth?" Mom asked, seething.

Bixia answered. "He escaped. When Marcus's hurricane weakened, I knew there was trouble. I found Marcus, Thomas and Simon unconscious inside the base." She shivered. "Cockroaches had them surrounded."

"They were protecting us," Marcus insisted.

Bixia wrinkled her nose and flicked her hands over her arms, searching for any remaining pesky roach passengers. "Whatever. There was no sign of Seth or his agents."

✠✠✠✠✠

Days passed. The fiery chasms in West Virginia and Nazca cooled. Wayne guessed the energy matter explosion successfully sealed the breaches and mended the E.M. realm. Selena and Helena worked on a plan to find Matthew and safely extract him from *Netherlandish Proverbs*. Seth's men remained jailed in Lady Brunel's painting, but Bixia provided them health breaks. During their meals Marcus probed their minds trying to uncover Seth's whereabouts and next scheme.

Alex spent most of the time in his room. Chasca and Olivia tried — unsuccessfully — to coax him into an unsanctioned trip to New York, and George used his Agate Talents to boost Alex spirits. It made his pain worse. Edward Devillin was the only visitor Alex welcomed. He didn't tell Alex to "do something fun to get your mind off Anne," or "be strong," or "give it time." Edward knew the pain of killing someone he loved.

Mom coped by losing herself in work, trying to use the rebirth spell on the Carnelian Tablet to improve pigments and stabilize Lady Brunel's portrait. She worked and slept in her lab, leaving Anne's bed untouched — Fosby Bear still resting on the pillow.

A week after the breach, Isadora returned to work. The burns Seth inflicted were still angry red. She offered to organize a memorial for Anne, but Mom couldn't face that — not yet. Alex was undecided. Part of him wanted to let her go. Maybe, one day, he would return to the Greenbrier ruins and try to contact her ghost.

While lying on his bed reading Mad Magazine, Alex heard his CyberNexus chime. Olivia: not interested, he decided. It chimed again: George. Alex rolled his eyes and pushed the device under his pillow. Five minutes later Chasca threw open his door. "Alex, come quickly! The energy spiders are back."

Thunder rumbled in the distance, as Alex followed Chasca through the dark halls to the transportation center. They pushed through the crowd to see energy spiders spinning a tightly woven web surrounding a black hole. In a bright flash of lightning, Bright Hand Wings arrived, filling the room. He held a cocoon of energy webbing in his claws.

The crowd drew back in fear, but Alex approached the beast. The Bat gently placed the webbing on the ground.

The Ooze trapped her in the core
when the Plexus's fabric tore.

Alex gasped in horror, tears welling in his eyes. The Bat had returned Anne's remains.

In peace the Plexus could be soon.
Thanks to Anne, the Ooze was strewn
to places where it won't balloon.

Rage built within Alex. He didn't care about the Plexus or the Bat anymore. "You killed her! You dropped her!"

Mom hurried to his side. "Is that Anne?"

"How do I take this stuff off her?" Alex asked, kneeling by Anne's body. "I want her out now!"

Bright Hand Wing looked at Anne's web sack.

The webbing will dissolve,
Then we'll see how she evolved.
Place her in seclusion.
Awakening creates confusion.

The energy spiders' webs faded as Bright Hand Wings took flight.

"Wait!" Alex called after him. "Does that mean she's . . ." He couldn't say the word aloud, couldn't bring himself to find hope again.

As the last of the thunder rumbled in the distance, the lights flickered on.

Alex turned to see his friends and other members of the Collective, watching him. "I think Anne's alive." Alex collapsed in tears next to Mom.

"How do we help her?" Elizabeth asked, hesitantly, as she held her son.

Alex tried to answer between sobs. "We have to move her . . . someplace quiet . . . before the webbing dissolves."

"The artifact room?" Isadora suggested.

"No!" Alex exclaimed. "I don't want her near that dodecahedron."

"Aunt Margaret's lake," Mom decided.

Alex's family and friends waited in Margaret's world for Anne to emerge from the cocoon. In less than an hour the webbing melted, leaving Anne's motionless body on the sandy beach. Her skin fluoresced as her body heaved to expel milky vomit from her mouth. Mom lifted Anne's head to keep her from choking.

Her eyes opened; she saw Mom and smiled. "You survived! And I'm awake." Her eyes grew heavy and closed.

"Is she okay?" Alex asked Helena.

Helena tried to rouse Anne. She remained unresponsive. "She has fallen into a coma. We should move her to somewhere comfortable and familiar."

"Take her to my room," Mom decided.

When Anne stirred two days later, Mom, Alex and Bakari were waiting. All three of them refused to leave her bedside. She looked radiant and peaceful — even if her skin fluoresced blue and gold.

"Anne, I'm so sorry, I thought I killed you," Alex confessed.

"Not yet," she said softly, "but I'm sure you will have more opportunities when we return to the Plexus."

Alex pulled back, revolted. "You can't! We have to find the Primal Key first. It's the only way to seal the time-tear."

She turned onto her side and clutched Fosby Bear. "But Alex, I'm the Primal Key."

Alex heard Anne's words, but all he could do was stare at her. He turned to Mom for answers, but she looked equally confused.

Anne spoke with greater strength. "At first I thought the owl from the Labyrinth was the Key. She helped me navigate the strings into the future. When I sicced the roaches on Seth to save Simon, I realized the owl was only a guide — I was and am the Key to morphing the future." She grabbed Alex's arm. "Say something — anything!"

A huge grin spread across Mom's face. "You saved Marcus and the strike team! How did you control the roaches?"

"I pictured Seth's dead, rotting corpse. The roaches did what came naturally to them. Did they kill Seth?"

"Seth," Mom spat his name, "escaped."

Alex cringed seeing Mom so angry.

"I guess Seth is too revolting — even for roaches." Bakari said, trying to lighten the mood. "So is your blue and gold tone permanent or should I ask Helena to work on a cure?"

"I need a different type of treatment and Bright Hand Wings needs a cure for the ooze."

"You can't go back to the Plexus!" Alex exclaimed. "You can't face the Gravity Lords! I can't face losing you again!"

"I must," Anne said gently. "When I hit the oozing river, I ignited the time-strings (your 'vibrating threads') with the energy matter. I splashed the ooze across the Plexus. It ran from me. All that was left was the charred ground of the E.M. riverbed. Instead of a big pool in the E.M. realm, now the ooze is spreading across all dimensions. Bright Hand Wings told me the Gravity Lords are furious. I polluted their realm, but it bought us more time to find a cure."

"A healing elixir?" Bakari asked. "One of the Onyx Tablet serums?"

"I don't know — yet," Anne replied, "but I'm the Primal Key and Alex is the Amalgamator. Together we'll find a way to stop the ooze. Right?"

"What happens if we don't do what the Bat wants?" Alex's stomach tightened into knots as he waited for her answer.

"The cure to rid the Plexus of the ooze — is also for me. When I touched the ooze, most of it fled, but a little made its way inside me. The Weaving Wave Riders — the energy spiders — revived me, but they can't remove the ooze. And they don't know what it will do to me."

Ever since Seth abducted Mom, Alex allowed anger, guilt and self-doubt to control him. He didn't feel confident — yet — but he was determined to find a cure for Anne. "I have the missing symbols for the Carnelian Tablet and you know all about the dodecahedron. We'll find a solution."

Anne sat up, some of her strength returning. "We need to deal with Seth, too. As long as he has the spheres, the Plexus and Earth are in danger."

"So where do we start?" Alex asked.

Anne's stomach rumbled. "Breakfast. I plan to eat my weight in pancakes. Want to come with?"

Alex smiled. "Of course. I told you, you're not allowed out of my sight." He helped her out of bed.

"Good!" Anne looped her arm through his. "While I eat, you can tell me all about Mom's rescue." She smiled at Bakari. "And I want to know what I missed at the Nazca Lines."

Made in the USA
Middletown, DE
08 March 2017